The Drama of Job

The Drama of Job

Burning Questions and Incomplete Answers

STEPHEN FINLAN

CASCADE *Books* · Eugene, Oregon

THE DRAMA OF JOB
Burning Questions and Incomplete Answers

Cascade Books
An Imprint of Wipf and Stock Publishers
199 W. 8th Ave., Suite 3
Eugene, OR 97401

www.wipfandstock.com

PAPERBACK ISBN: 978-1-6667-7233-3
HARDCOVER ISBN: 978-1-6667-7234-0
EBOOK ISBN: 978-1-6667-7235-7

Cataloguing-in-Publication data:

Names: Finlan, Stephen.

Title: The drama of Job : burning questions and incomplete answers / Stephen
Finlan.

Description: Eugene, OR: Cascade Books, 2025 | Includes bibliographical refer-
ences and index.

Identifiers: ISBN 978-1-6667-7233-3 (paperback) | ISBN 978-1-6667-7234-0
(hardcover) | ISBN 978-1-6667-7235-7 (ebook)

Subjects: LCSH: Bible. Job—Criticism, interpretation, etc. | Elihu (biblical
figure) | Bible plays

Classification: BS1415.52 .F55 2025 (paperback) | BS1415.52 (ebook)

VERSION NUMBER 03/17/25

Contents

Abbreviations

ANE	Ancient Near East[ern]
ASV	American Standard Version
BDB	*The New Brown, Driver, and Briggs Hebrew and English Lexicon of the Old Testament*
CBQ	*Catholic Biblical Quarterly*
JBL	*Journal of Biblical Literature*
HCSB	Holman Christian Standard Bible
KJV	King James Version
LXX	The Septuagint (Greek translation of the Hebrew Bible, third to second centuries BCE)
MT	Masoretic Text (Hebrew text)
NABRE	New American Bible, Revised Edition
NASB	New American Standard Bible
NCV	New Century Version
NICOT	New International Commentary on the Old Testament
NIV	New International Version
NRSV	New Revised Standard Version
NT	New Testament
OTP	*Old Testament Pseudepigrapha*, edited by James Charlesworth
WBC	Word Biblical Commentary
WJK	Westminster John Knox

Introduction

W ho among us is not drawn to heroes? What compels them to go forward when all seems lost? Job is a heroic character because he courageously questions the standard theology of his day, and demands better answers to the problem of suffering than his conformist "friends" can offer. He is not satisfied with their conventional answer that the righteous never suffer calamities, so that Job must have sinned, if he is now suffering. Job knows this simple answer is inadequate, and he will not stop until he finds a better answer. He will demand it even from God.

My approach is literary, theological, and historical-critical. I consider many differing approaches by scholars, while constructing my own synthesis.

HOSTILITY TO ELIHU

As the enemy of conformity and passivity, Job appeals to modern sensibilities. But there is another hero in the book of Job, one who gets beyond conformity and nonconformity alike: This is Elihu, the sage who interrupts the debate between Job and his moralistic friends, and delivers a long monologue in chapters 32–37. The majority of scholarship vilifies Elihu, considering him an unhelpful critic like the "friends," or even identifying him with the satan who appears in the first two chapters. William Whedbee calls him "a buffoon."[1] Edwin Good sees Elihu as "insufferably pompous"[2] and "depressingly conventional . . . wordy, convoluted."[3] Roger Norman Whybray calls him "a fool."[4]

There are legitimate reasons for the scholarly hostility to Elihu. The Elihu character interrupts the dramatic flow; he is self-assured, wordy, and stern towards Job. Most scholars have allowed their annoyance with Elihu's style to blind them to the content of his teaching. Notable exceptions to this attitude are Carol Newsom,[5] John Hartley,[6] Stephen Vicchio,[7] and David Clines.[8]

Negative opinions about Elihu go back to the early centuries. The Greek apocryphal work, the *Testament of Job*, treats Elihu as a "Satanic beast." Among Christian interpreters, Gregory the Great conceded that Elihu understood Job's problem, but said his words were "proud and arrogant."[9]

But Elihu expresses ideas not heard from any of the other characters in the book. Job and the friends are concerned only with questions of justice and recompense, while Yahweh, at the end of the book, is concerned with spelling out how limited is human understanding and how puny is human power. Only Elihu puts the emphasis on God's mercy, on his varied and energetic attempts to reach and rescue people: "God speaks in one way, and in two. . . . In a dream, in a vision of the night, when deep sleep falls on mortals . . . that he may turn them aside from their deeds, and keep them from pride, to spare their souls from the Pit" (Job 33:14–18). If there is one "angel, a mediator, one of a thousand" to intervene for a person, to call for his deliverance, "then he prays to God, and is accepted by him" (33:23, 26).

1. Whedbee, "Comedy of Job," 28.

2. Good, *In Turns of Tempest*, 326.

3. Good, *In Turns of Tempest*, 337.

4. Whybray, *Job*, 139.

5. Newsom, *Book of Job*, 209–22, for instance.

6. Hartley, *Book of Job*, 446–50, 483–86, for instance.

7. Vicchio, *Job*, 212–14, 248, for instance.

8. Clines, *Job 21–37*, 724–43, 854–56, for instance.

9. Vicchio, *Job*, 216.

I have written a somewhat playful and unorthodox stage play that reenacts the Job story, but makes Elihu the main hero. That is the Appendix to this work. Despite its playfulness, I am serious about raising up what is spiritually useful in Elihu's teachings. In the book of Job as we have it, Elihu is important intellectually, but he is not important narratively. None of the other characters take any notice of him, and he has no effect on Job's attitude. In my play, I have made Elihu important narratively and dramatically.

THE COMPOSITION AND ANTIQUITY OF THE BOOK

The book of Job could be considered part of a genre or category of Ancient Near Eastern literature concerned with theodicy. Theodicy means reflection about why God allows evil (*literally* it means "justifying God," in the sense of justifying the *ways* of God). The theodical discussions we find in Job are unique. It is the framework of Job—the prose setup in chapters 1–2, the Yahweh-Job Dialogue in 38:1—42:6, and the prose narrative at the end in 42:7–17—that finds some Mesopotamian ancestors.

The end of the book has Yahweh answering (actually *not* answering) Job's questions, putting Job in his place, overwhelming him with comments about creation, ultimately shutting down Job's questioning and implied criticism, but also rejecting the approach of the three friends, and finally vindicating Job and restoring health and wealth to him.

The framing chapters somewhat resemble a Mesopotamian work called either *A Poem of a Righteous Sufferer* or "I Will Praise the Lord of Wisdom," *Ludlul Bēl Nēmeqi*, known "from the library of Ashurbanipal (669–33 B.C.)," although "the date of composition . . . goes back to Cassite times (1600–1150 B.C.)."[10] In that work, a righteous worshipper of Marduk loses everything, becomes sick, laments his fate, prays to Marduk, and has his wealth and health restored.[11] While suffering, he sees four visions. In the

10. Pope, *Job*, xxxiii.
11. Margulies, "Oh That One," 584–85.

third vision, he is comforted by a woman who looks like a goddess and tells him he will be delivered. In the fourth vision, a sage visits him and heals him.[12]

What makes the book of Job so interesting—the long debate about evil and about God's justice—is precisely what is *not* present in "I Will Praise the Lord of Wisdom." That work pictures a righteous man suffering, and has some superficial resemblance to Job 1–2 and 42, but it has none of Job's prolonged questioning of the *reason* for the suffering of the innocent. Another key difference is in the main character's argumentation: the Mesopotamian hero "stresses his ritual piety, Job his ethical probity."[13] The Babylonian text might be a literary influence upon the framing chapters of the book of Job, but the Hebrew book as we have it is decidedly unique and differs importantly from any Babylonian predecessors.

Another Babylonian text bears some resemblance to Job. This is an acrostic poem known as the *Babylonian Theodicy*, hailing from the eleventh century BCE existing in Neo-Assyrian and Neo-Babylonian. It is a debate between a sufferer and a debate partner over retribution theology.[14] Many of the phrases, intriguingly, sound like phrases from Job, but not enough to prove a direct literary influence.[15] The sufferer bemoans that the wicked are not punished. His partner rebukes that view, and at the end, the sufferer suddenly and surprisingly backs down and accepts the traditional opinion.[16]

There also are some suggestions of Egyptian religious ideas. The idea of the heart being weighed in a balance (31:6) echoes a scene in the Egyptian *Book of the Dead*.[17] The recital of good deeds in 29:1–24 also echoes a similar list in the *Book of the Dead*.[18] But especially does the image of a new tree sprouting up from a

12. Adams, *Redefining Job*, 141.

13. Pope, *Job*, lxiv.

14. Moore, *Retribution*, 84–91.

15. Andersen, *Job*, 29–30.

16. Margulies, "Oh That One," 587–88.

17. Hays, "There Is Hope for a Tree," 57.

18. Hays, "There Is Hope for a Tree," 62–63.

stump (14:7–9) reflect Egyptian ideas of an afterlife.[19] This will be addressed in the sequential interpretation, in the next chapter.

Further, there are some Egyptian works of literature that bear some resemblances to Job. *The Dialogue of Ipu-Wer with the Lord of All* not only complains about robbery and greed, but blames the deity—apparently Ra—for not doing something about it:[20] "Look, why does he create people without distinguishing between the gentle and the violent? . . . Where is he today? Is he asleep?"[21] The ties with Mesopotamian literature seem to be more numerous and unmistakable, but the author of Job may have had some familiarity with Egyptian literature, too.

Many scholars believe the prose framework was composed first, and the Dialogue inserted later. Gerhard von Rad writes, "The oldest layer, the narrative prose framework (Job i–ii, xlii. 7–11), is of course to be considered separately, for it would be a mistake to try to understand it against the background of a deeply shaken faith,"[22] meaning the shaken faith of Job in the Dialogue. He sees the Dialogue being added "perhaps several hundred years later" than the composition of "the pre-exilic prose narrative."[23] Margulies stresses the serious incompatibility in theology between Job 1–2, 38–42 and the Dialogue chapters 3–31 (minus chapter 28), which leads him to assert different authorship for the two main parts of Job. "Does Job patiently accept his misfortune, as he does in the prose tale, or does he reject this teaching and rage furiously against tradition and accepted wisdom" as he does in the Dialogue?[24] "It appears that the dialogue, extending from chapter 3 to chapter 31 (excluding 28), existed as its own independent document prior to its incorporation into the Book of Job."[25] I will return to this issue in the sequential section, after considering chapter 31.

19. Hays, "There Is Hope for a Tree," 43–55, 60, 66–68.

20. Moore, *Retribution*, 80–81.

21. Moore, *Retribution*, 82.

22. Rad, *Old Testament*, 408.

23. Rad, *Old Testament*, 409.

24. Margulies, "Oh That One," 585.

25. Margulies, "Oh That One," 599.

The language and syntax of the text are usually the determinative factors in scholars' estimates placing the book "between the sixth and fourth centuries."[26] "The Israeli scholar Y. Kaufmann contends for a pre-exilic date for Job ... The antiquity of the prose framework, Kaufmann feels, is vouched for by its highly naïve images of God."[27] Andersen proposes a pre-exilic date for the book, "with the age of Solomon as a real, but perhaps the earliest, possibility."[28] Pope thinks "the seventh century BCE seems the best guess for the date of the Dialogue."[29]

Several other data contribute to the argument for multiple authorship. The Prologue and Epilogue use the names Yahweh and Elohim, while the Dialogue "employs variously the terms El, Eloah, Elohim, and Shaddai. The temper and mood of the Prologue-Epilogue and of the Dialogue are quite distinct." The Dialogue "is highly charged with emotion," while the prose framework is not.[30] "Most critics ... regard the Prologue-Epilogue as part of an ancient folk tale which the author of the Dialogue used as the framework and point of departure for his poetic treatment of the problem of suffering."[31]

This assessment makes sense. The prose frame of Job echoes the deprival and restoration theme found in *Ludlul Bēl Nēmeqi*. On the other hand, Job's argumentativeness in the Dialogue followed by a sudden relenting do echo those elements found in *Babylonian Theodicy*. It seems likely that the prose frame of Job existed, and someone who read it found it deeply unsatisfying, writing the Dialogue of chapters 3–31 to challenge the providential theology, but left the frame intact, perhaps to protect the expanded version from conservative attacks and allow it still to be considered acceptable for reading. Most likely, chapter 28, a reflection on Wisdom, was added later, as were the Elihu chapters 32–37.

---

26. Pope, *Job*, xxxiv.

27. Pope, *Job*, xxxviii, citing Kaufmann, *Religion of Israel*, 334–38.

28. Andersen, *Job*, 60, 64.

29. Pope, *Job*, xliii.

30. Pope, *Job*, xxiv.

31. Pope, *Job*, xxiv.

A different view is advocated by Israel McGrew, who sees the Dialogue chapters as anticipating the book's conclusion. McGrew resists the idea that the poet used Job as the mouthpiece of his own views, setting Job's own statements in opposition to the theology of the final chapters. McGrew sees the Job Dialogue and the poetic Yahweh speech as being written by the same author. "We cannot merely identify Job as the poet's mouthpiece and allow him to carry the day against the narrative, as the poet himself has left us to contend with the speech from the whirlwind."[32]

While McGrew's argument is interesting, and he certainly is right to point to "the complexities" of the book of Job, it seems a stretch for him to argue that the author actually rejects much of what he has Job saying. For instance, "Job's parody of Psalm 8 is self-defeating."[33] In effect, he is saying that the author is repudiating the things that Job says, while affirming the things that Job criticizes or mocks. It is not convincing to speak of "the poet's strategy in alluding to, parodying, and ultimately vindicating traditional, pious speech."[34] McGrew seems to be forcibly harmonizing Job's words with the theology of the Prologue and Epilogue.

I think that the authors of the Dialogue and of the Elihu monologue both knew of, and were willing to keep in place, the more conservative views of the Prologue and Epilogue. Elihu, in particular, seems to anticipate and echo Yahweh's speeches at the end of his own speech (36:26—37:23), perhaps in order to reduce any perceived incongruity between his speech and Yahweh's.

Some of the older scholars took note of the strange and ancient literary tropes found throughout Job, and speculated on its antiquity. More recent scholars tend to downplay these signs of antiquity and focus on syntax and vocabulary, insisting that the book fits into the Persian Period on lexical grounds, perhaps 500 to 375 BCE. I accept some parts of both arguments. I think Job is a layered work, and that its oldest layers are many centuries older than the Persian Period of the final redaction. There are no extant

---

32. McGrew, "'What is Enosh?'" 416.

33. McGrew, "'What is Enosh?'" 422.

34. McGrew, "'What is Enosh?'" 418.

manuscripts enabling me to prove the existence of earlier layers of Job. I have to base my argument upon content, upon the primitive rustic setting, the dominance of naturalistic elements, and on the naïve theological ideas and mythological imagery occurring throughout the book.

I am highly skeptical of attempts to link the book's theme to Judah's national humiliation. There is no hint of national suffering or destiny in Job, of the loss of temple, priesthood, of election, "Zion," covenant, or kingship. In fact, when Job offers sacrifice, he does it himself without any priest (1:5). Likewise, Eliphaz and the friends are told to go and offer up sacrifices "for yourselves" (42:8). Priesthood and temple are never mentioned. The Hebrew monarchies and wars go unmentioned.

The story seems to picture Job and his friends as Edomites.[35] The land of Uz (1:1) is assigned to Edom by Lamentations 4:21. Teman, from whence Job's friend Eliphaz hails, is in Edom (Jer 49:7, 20; Ezek 25:13; Amos 1:11–12).[36] Eliphaz and the other friends seem to have names that are Edomite or southern Semitic.[37] The gentile setting of the story pictures suffering as a universal experience, unrelated to political and national events. If the political fate of Judah were the real underpinning of the story, we would expect at least some trace of the standard answers for the exile that we see in the prophetic and Deuteronomistic traditions (betrayal of the covenant, giving in to Baalist temptations, the threat of a "day of the Lord,"[38] impure or immoral priests and kings, needing to be exiled in order to be taught a lesson, and so on). And it is hard to imagine an exilic or postexilic author choosing Edomites as main characters, given the Edomite exploitation of Judah, and "the overwhelmingly vitriolic response to Edom in exilic and postexilic literature."[39]

---

35. Gordis, *Book of God*, 115. There are a few scholarly dissenters from this tentative conclusion. Boss mentions other scholarly guesses: Syria or Arabia (*Human Consciousness*, 16).

36. Andersen, *Job*, 99.

37. Gordis, *Book of God*, 115.

38. Terrien, "Job as a Sage," 240.

39. Anderson, "Edom's (Dis)Possession," 376. Scholars debate whether

Instead, the book endeavors to find theological answers to old questions, attacking a shallow and conventional theology that says earthly prosperity is always a direct result of one's righteousness. Both the frequent presence of mythological elements in the Dialogue and the absence of common prophetic concepts (such as covenant; a law written on the heart; messianic hopes of various kinds) point to the book's antiquity.

The book is a *philosophical*, not a *political*, reflection. Job's suffering is personal and existential, not related to the fate of Judah, Israel, or Edom. It is *human* suffering that is in view: "Do not human beings have a hard service on earth?" (7:1). The book of Job concerns personal piety, experienced calamity, and concepts of divine justice. The core of the book is the character Job's sharp rejection of the belief that suffering and calamity are evidence of God's disfavor, or that wealth and health show that one is favored by God. In some ways, the book is a hero's journey. The drama is provided by the staunch but opposing views of Job and his friends.

Michael Moore says there is a clear philosophic question at the book's basis: "the Prologue introduces the book of Job by forthrightly stating its central polarity—*retribution* vs. *reality*. Is God to be served only to receive a reward or avoid punishment? Or is he to be served without preconditions because he is God, the Sovereign Lord?"[40] "The key tension [is] *compensation/retribution* vs. *disinterested piety*."[41] James Crenshaw makes a further point. He argues that "the cynical charge that Job's piety depended upon favorable external circumstances struck at the heart of ancient religion . . . It follows that innocent suffering functions as a *secondary* theme of the story."[42] However, even if innocent suffering is logically secondary, it becomes a primary concern as regards the space it takes up within the Dialogue. I think one could say that disinterested piety

---

Edom participated in the conquest of Judah in 587 BCE, but all recognize "the growth of anti-Edom rhetoric following the downfall of Judah and Jerusalem" (Anderson, "Edom's (Dis)Possession," 382).

40. Moore, *Retribution*, 34.

41. Moore, *Retribution*, 69.

42. Crenshaw, *Old Testament Wisdom*, 100–101.

is the basic question raised by the Prologue, but the Dialogue raises many questions about the suffering of the innocent, how to relate to God during times of suffering, the prospering of the wicked, and the question of whether the wicked always get their comeuppance in this lifetime. The Dialogue's drama is not *entirely* centered upon the question of disinterested piety raised by the Prologue.

Scholars have wrestled with the question of whether the Dialogue in Job fits the genre of a stage play. Suggestions that Job is an imitation of Greek drama or of a Platonic dialogue have not convinced many.[43] One scholar opines that, in Greek tragedy, "fate . . . dictat[es] the ways both of God and men," thus lacking the "genuine dramatic suspense in Job."[44] The eighteenth century scholar R. Lowth concluded that it lacks the action that characterizes stage plays, but that it has elements of drama and could even be characterized as a "dramatic poem."[45]

JOB, THE HERO OF HONEST FAITH

The author who created this brave nonconformist character gives us one of the world's greatest works of intellectual drama.

Job has been called an example of endurance (James 5:11). If endurance means seeking the truth even at the cost of being labeled impious by a self-righteous majority, then Job is indeed an example of endurance. But, in fact, the Job character expresses fatigue with having to endure suffering, and is quite confrontational in some of his rhetoric.

The book of Job is a sharp critique of the belief that one's earthly status reflects God's favor or disfavor, that the righteous are always rewarded and the wicked always punished in *this* lifetime, and that anyone who is suffering must have done some evil. This simplistic and harsh theology, sometimes called providence theology, makes God the cause of everything that happens. The

43. Andersen, *Job*, 36–37.

44. Kaufmann, "Expostulation," 67.

45. Cited in Andersen, *Job*, 36.

only way for the author to challenge this thesis is by studying the case of a righteous person who is made to suffer, and that is what the character Job embodies. The plot device of a bet between God and the satan, in which God agrees to let the satan take away Job's children, wealth, and health (but not his hectoring wife! [2:9]), sets up the situation of a just man suffering.

Job repeatedly asks to appear before God. This is a theme we sometimes see in the Psalms: "My soul thirsts for God, for the living God. When shall I come and behold the face of God?" (Ps 42:2). "One thing I asked of the Lord, that will I seek after: to live in the house of the Lord all the days of my life, to behold the beauty of the Lord, and to inquire in his temple" (Ps 27:4).

In an unusual view, Terence Tilley has asserted that the book of Job is not about theodicy at all. He makes a valid point when he says that theodicy can be a "solution" that creates problems.[46] Tilley is outraged by inadequate answers, rationalizations, and arguments that are far removed from concrete instances of human suffering. Theodicy can amount to "consoling doctrines" that are merely "the propositional ingredient in immoral actions of repression and subjugation."[47]

I would argue that theodicy, like *any* kind of theology, can be bent to evil purposes. But, *contra* Tilley, it is not *always* twisted to such ends. Tilley asserts that, because theodicy does not talk about systems of evil, it therefore "propagates more evil than it explains by effectively erasing structural evils."[48] But theodicy can definitely address the question of systemic evil on the human level. And the Job character touches upon organized evil when he says "Why do the wicked . . . grow mighty in power? . . . The plans of the wicked are repugnant to me" (21:7, 16). "There are those who snatch the orphan child from the breast, and take as a pledge the infant of the poor" (24:9). The author is not ignorant of the fact that these seizures are an organized effort carried out by powerful people.

---

46. Tilley, *Evils of Theodicy*, 1; and see 109.

47. Tilley, *Evils of Theodicy*, 4.

48. Tilley, "Trajectory of Positions," 181.

Further, I simply have to disagree with Tilley's premise that "Theodicy proper is a modern undertaking."[49] The *word* may be modern,[50] but the endeavor is at least as old as the *Babylonian Theodicy*. Tilley argues that the real quest of the Job character is for an encounter with God. I don't think that needs to be set against the fact that Job is *also* seeking to understand why the wicked prosper and the just suffer. The positive assertions Tilley makes about Job's quest for encounter are valid, but they need not be used to deny the presence of theodicy.

I can moderate my criticism of Tilley when I take note of the distinction he makes between a "defence" and a "theodicy."[51] He sees a "defence" as a legitimate argument for the reality of God despite the reality of evil,[52] while a theodicy attempts to *explain* the inexplicable.[53] "There is no explanation for evil."[54] This is not a very precise distinction, and many things that Tilley calls "defences," others would call "theodicies." He does not reject all attempts to defend the goodness of God. It seems that what he is mostly (and legitimately) upset with are theodical explanations that provide "pat" and simplistic answers to difficult questions; that attempt to shut down the discussion with pompous claims to solve the problem. He seems to be saying that *all* explanations are inadequate, which I think is one-sided and overstates the problem. I would argue that there are many partial explanations, some of which Tilley would call "defences," and that many of them have some (limited) intellectual and spiritual value. Theodicy is not synonymous with arrogance and dogmatism, although there are arrogant and dogmatic versions of it.

---

49. Tilley, *Evils of Theodicy*, 2.

50. Coined by Leibniz in 1710; Tilley, *Evils of Theodicy*, 2.

51. Evidently a distinction made by Plantinga; see Adams, *Horrendous Evils*, 178n26.

52. Tilley, "Trajectory of Positions," 188.

53. Tilley, *Evils of Theodicy*, 1.

54. Tilley, "Reply to Nagasawa," 199.

Moore insists that theodicy is a secondary theme, and that the main issue in the book is "disinterested piety,"[55] whether Job worships God independently of his earthly prosperity, or whether he worships only because of the benefits he gets.[56] This is a challenge to religious piety itself, to *any* person's reason for worshipping. Job seems to pass this test successfully, thus enabling God to win the argument against the satan.

Unaware of the heavenly council, Job struggles to understand the reason for his suffering, whether God has become hostile to him, and whether God is fair. Thus, it fundamentally *does* deal with the issue of theodicy, in my opinion. Why does God allow this to happen? How do I reconcile this with the goodness and justice of God? These are the basic questions of theodicy, and it *is* a central theme of the book of Job. Except in the first two chapters, the answer is *not* "because God took a bet and allowed an innocent person to be tormented." The answers (and partial answers) given throughout the rest of the book of Job do not have to do with a heavenly wager, but with questions about the goodness of God (theodicy), and also about piety during times of suffering.

55. Moore, *Retribution*, 9, agreeing with Moberly (*Bible*, 85–86), Newsom (*Book of Job*, 50, 181), and Seow (*Job 1–21*, 262–63).

56. Moore, *Retribution*, 10.

1

Sequential Exploration
of the Debate

Proceeding chapter by chapter, we see that debate constitutes the majority of the book. Speeches and debates take up chapters 3 through 42:6. That portion, the majority of the book, closely resembles a stage play, but first it is set up by a narrative framework.

There are many textual problems and confusions with the Hebrew text. "The Book of Job is textually the most vexed in the Old Testament."[1] Often, however, the basic arguments are clear, even when some of the imagery and vocabulary are debatable.

THE FRAMEWORK

Chapters 1–2 and 42:7–17 provide a narrative framework for the Dialogue. The narrator begins by describing Job as "blameless and upright" (1:1), and this is confirmed in the same words by Yahweh in 1:8 and 2:3. "Blameless" could also be translated "perfect." The word is *tam*, the same word used in the Siloam inscription, marking the breakthrough in the digging of the tunnel for the spring of Jerusalem.[2]

---

1. Pope, *Job*, xlii.
2. Boss, *Human Consciousness*, 16.

The setting of the drama is the heavenly council, when the "heavenly beings" (NRSV) or "the sons of God came to present themselves before the Lord, the satan also came among them" (Job 1:6 NABRE). The term translated "heavenly beings" by the NRSV, *bene ha-elohim*, is quite literally "sons of God" or "sons of the gods," probably the same as "the council of the holy ones" (Ps 89:7), and possibly "the angels of later theology,"[3] or the "host of heaven" as at 1 Kings 22:19, the latter leading to the divine name "the Lord of hosts" (Isa 37:32; 54:5). The influential philosopher Philo of Alexandria thought the *bene ha-elohim* were cherubim. The important medieval Jewish writer Rashi thought they were "angelic Lords, the sons of lords and judges."[4] Coming "among" the sons of God is "the satan" (*ha-satan*), as NABRE translates the next term, although most other translations render it as the proper name Satan. The word comes from the Semitic root for "adversary" or "accuser," and it has forms as an adjective, a noun, or a verb in the Hebrew Bible.[5] Moore insists that it cannot be a proper name here, since it is prefixed by the definite article, and it simply means "the prosecutor."[6] Although the satan takes on an adversarial role in Job, he has not yet become the demonic figure that he would be in the New Testament. However, Andersen seems correct to say: "His insolence shows a mind already twisted away from God, but his hostility is not on the scale of a rival power."[7] Andersen says he is theologically unimportant in the book of Job. None of the characters in Job attribute human suffering to a devil.[8]

The satan shows up "among" the "heavenly beings," having been roaming the world (1:6–7). The Lord more or less brags about his servant Job, whom he calls blameless (1:8). The satan's skeptical reply is that Job has been protected and blessed in all ways, but if these protections are withdrawn "he will curse you to your face"

3. Andersen, *Job*, 296; see also Boss, *Human Consciousness*, 25.

4. Vicchio, *Job*, 50.

5. Vicchio, *Job*, 51.

6. Moore, *Retribution*, 23.

7. Andersen, *Job*, 87.

8. Andersen, *Job*, 88.

(1:11). The Lord tells the satan "Very well, all that he has is in your power," except that he may not kill him (1:12). What quickly follows are the theft of his donkeys and oxen by raiders, a fire that burns up his sheep and servants, another raid that takes away his camels and kills more servants, and then a wind that destroys his house and kills all his children (1:13–19). Job's reply is the famous "Naked I came from my mother's womb, and naked shall I return there; the Lord gave, and the Lord has taken away; blessed be the name of the Lord." (1:21). This shows his continuing righteousness: "In all this Job did not sin or charge God with wrongdoing" (1:22).

This calamity is not enough, as far as the satan is concerned, "But stretch out your hand now and touch his bone and his flesh, and he will curse you to your face" (2:5). The satan then is allowed to afflict Job with sores from head to foot (2:7). There may be echoes of Deuteronomy in Job. His being afflicted with sores (2:7) seems to echo the threat of Deuteronomy 28:35: "The Lord will strike you . . . with grievous boils." The "dread" that befalls him in Job 3:25 may fulfill the threat in Deuteronomy 28:60: "He will bring back upon you all the diseases of Egypt, of which you were in dread, and they shall cling to you."[9] These indicate a date of composition after Deuteronomy (approx. 620 BCE), but I have already accepted that the book's latest recension may date from the sixth or fifth century BCE. This does not negate the possibility of its main composition taking place considerably earlier.

The next action is a negative comment by Job's wife: "Do you still persist in your integrity [*tummah*]? Curse God, and die," but he refuses to do so (2:9–10). One could discern an element of dark comedy in this single line that the wife gets. Some interpreters understand the wife's comment in a more positive light. The word *barach* can mean either bless or curse, and Bernard of Clairvaux thought she was saying "bless God and die," as did the philosopher Martin Buber.[10] Job's rebuke and rejoinder in the next verse, however ("foolish woman"), seem to suggest that cursing was intended, and that Job refuses to take the suggestion. He answers that we

9. Kynes and Kynes, *Wrestling with Job*, 150.

10. Vicchio, *Job*, 58–59, 63.

have to accept both good and bad from the Lord's hand, which the author characterizes as a sinless answer (2:10).

Job's three friends come to "console and comfort him" (2:11), and they sit with him in silence for seven days (2:13). They should have remained silent, for when they finally do speak, their words don't even come up to the level of cold comfort.

THE DEBATE WITH THE FRIENDS

The First Round

The drama begins as Job, deprived of progeny and prospects, is sitting in ashes, scraping his skins lesions with a potsherd (2:8), and is joined by the three friends, who represent conformity to the providence theology popular in their culture.

Job starts by cursing the day he was born, showing us that his suffering is intense (3:3–26). He seeks rest and release for the weary at 3:17, 26, "likely referring to the ultimate 'rest' of death."[11] The dead are "quiet" and "at ease" (3:13, 18), having no more "trouble" (v. 17), which may mean that the dead are in a semi-conscious condition. The cursing of his "day" shows the intensity of Job's "groanings" and "troubles" (3:24, 26). He does not enumerate his particular losses, but he regrets ever having been born. It is an emotionally powerful lament.[12]

Eliphaz the Temanite gives the first response to Job. He starts off politely, but before long he is stressing that the innocent don't suffer: "Who that was innocent ever perished? Or where were the upright cut off?" (4:7). Instead, "those who plough iniquity and sow trouble reap the same" (4:8), implying that Job must have done some evil. Eliphaz shares a frightening night vision he has had (4:12–16), in which a voice asked: "Can mortals be righteous before God? ... Even in his servants he puts no trust, and his angels he charges with error; how much more those who live in

11. Kynes and Kynes, *Wrestling with Job*, 54.

12. Moore notices important similarities to Jeremiah's lament, cursing the day of his birth (20:14), lamenting the "toil and sorrow" of his life (20:18) (Moore, *Retribution*, 119–20).

houses of clay" (4:17–19). People are short-lived, and "they die devoid of wisdom" (4:21). Job is foolish to complain: "Surely vexation kills the fool, and jealousy slays the simple" (5:2). The teaching combines pessimism ("human beings are born to trouble," 5:7) and optimism: if Job commits his cause to God, God will rescue him (5:8, 15–26). Further, he should take the Lord's discipline as helpful: "How happy is the one whom God reproves; therefore do not despise the discipline of the Almighty. For he wounds, but he binds up" (5:17–18). This can be called the "moral qualities view," the idea that sufferings are meant to teach moral qualities.[13] It also is quite *moralistic*, in that it is pompous and lacks sympathy. The problem is the way that it imagines "a predictable (and that means, to some extent, manageable) God."[14]

This rosy picture provides no comfort for Job, who is not really seeking restoration of his previous status, but restoration of his relationship to God in his *present circumstances*. He feels persecuted by God: "the arrows of the Almighty are in me" (6:4). Job is not just wrestling with his fate, he is arguing with the *interpretation* of his fate by the self-satisfied representatives of conformity: "Teach me, and I will be silent; make me understand how I have gone wrong. . . . But your reproof, what does it reprove?" (6:24–25); he has done no wrong: "Is there any wrong on my tongue?" (6:30).

Job then identifies his suffering with the common human suffering: "Do not human beings have a hard service on earth, and are not their days like the days of a laborer? Like a slave who longs for the shadow" (7:1–2). But then, his lot is worse than most. His flesh is dirty and it breaks out (7:5); he might die without hope (7:6). The gloomy concept of Sheol is affirmed: "those who go down to Sheol do not come up" (7:9).[15] Job speaks out of anguish; "I will complain in the bitterness of my soul" (7:11). Job is longing for more than the rest of death; he is seeking consolation (*nakham*): "my bed will comfort me" (7:13).[16]

---

13. Vicchio, *Job*, 397.

14. Andersen, *Job*, 134.

15. Emphasizing the continuity with Babylonian beliefs: Vicchio, *Job*, 74.

16. Kynes and Kynes, *Wrestling with Job*, 55.

Job gives what looks like an ironic reversal of Psalm 8:4–5. The latter asks "what are human beings that you are mindful of them, mortals that you care for them? Yet you have made them a little lower than God, and crowned them with glory and honor." The psalmist notes our mortality, but also our amazing status, a little lower than God. Job keeps the opening question, but creates a second one that dwells on God's hounding of the individual: "What are human beings, that you make so much of them, that you set your mind on them, visit them every morning, test them every moment?" (7:17–18). He takes the psalm's expression of wonder and satirically turns it into a complaint. The verb *pāqad*, usually meaning "visit," has the sense "care for" in Psalm 8:4, but has the tone of "a punitive" visit in Job 7:18.[17]

Job's argument is not just with the friends, but with God (really with the *concept* of God that is assumed). He feels persecuted by this God, and begs "Let me alone, for my days are a breath . . . Will you not look away from me for a while, let me alone until I swallow my spittle?" (7:16, 19). He is baffled by God's apparent cruelty. What harm can he really do to God? "If I sin, what do I do to you, you watcher of humanity? Why have you made me your target?" (7:20).

The three friends talk *about* God, but Job talks *to* God, and with passion and honesty.[18] His efforts will pay off in the end, when God makes an appearance from a whirlwind. Presumably the author empathizes with Job's questions, with his worry. Job does not mourn for his family and servants or for his loss of wealth. He seems most upset by his apparently damaged relationship to God. He is most worked up about God's apparent attitude toward him. Later on, he will reminisce about his lost "prime, when the friendship of God was upon my tent" (29:4).

Job's frustration is not surprising. "He knows that what he is experiencing from God is not a true reflection of who he knows

---

17. Good, *Irony*, 227.

18. "Job is dreadfully in earnest" (Andersen, *Job*, 104); see also Boss, *Human Consciousness*, 219.

God to be."[19] Or, stated more starkly: "All Job has known about God he still believes. But God's inexplicable ways have his mind perplexed to breaking point."[20]

Job's stance is one of "defiant faith . . . a type of pious protest,"[21] arguing with God as also do a number of the lament Psalms and other books of the Bible. Complaint does not lead to atheism, but to further complaint, petitioning, and sometimes to an expression of trust and faith. An Abraham or a Moses could persuade God to change his course (Gen 18:20–32; Exod 32:11–14). Maybe Job can persuade God to explain why Job is being punished.

But his interlocutors do not see him as a loyal debater with God. Bildad the Shuhite scolds him, saying "if you are pure and upright, surely then he will rouse himself for you and restore to you your rightful place" (8:6). It is the godless who suffer (8:12–14). In fact, Bildad is crude enough to say that, if Job's children sinned, then God "delivered them into the power of their transgression" (8:4). Bildad insists "God will not reject a blameless person" (8:20).

Job accepts this principle, and admits that he cannot contend with God (9:2–3) the Creator, who is great beyond Job's knowing (9:9–10), but he repeats that he is innocent (9:15, 21). In fact, *God* knows "that I am not guilty" (10:7). Pessimistically, he concludes that God "destroys both the blameless and the wicked" (9:22), and he yearns for a mediator or an "umpire between us" (9:33) so he could talk to God "without fear of him" (9:35). He begs God "let me know why you contend against me" (10:2). God created him, and even "granted me life and steadfast love, and your care has preserved my spirit" (10:12), which makes it all the more baffling that "now you turn and destroy me" (10:8) and "watch me" in a judgmental way (10:14). More optimistically, one could say Job is realizing "that he has worth also in being God's handiwork."[22] But the pessimism persists. Job can only look forward to descent to the underworld, "the land of gloom and chaos, where light is like

19. Kynes and Kynes, *Wrestling with Job*, 87.

20. Andersen, *Job*, 150.

21. Kynes and Kynes, *Wrestling with Job*, 152.

22. Boss, *Human Consciousness*, 73.

darkness" (10:22). This reflects the commonly held theology about the gloomy half-awake condition of the afterlife. Job even anticipates the self-abasement that he will express when he encounters Yahweh near the end of the book: "How then can I answer him . . . I do not know myself; I loathe my life" (9:14, 21; 10:1).

Job's claim to be "not guilty" (10:7) really gets on the nerves of the third friend, Zophar the Naamathite: "For you say, 'My conduct is pure, and I am clean in God's sight'" (11:4). Zophar implies that Job has gotten off lightly for "your guilt" (11:6). Even Job's questions are disturbing to this conformist, who asks "Can you find out the deep things of God?" (11:7). He considers Job arrogant, but also stupid, like a wild ass (11:12). Zophar is harsher than Eliphaz and Bildad.[23] He finishes by saying that only if Job removes iniquity from "your hand," then "you will forget your misery . . . and your life will be brighter than the noonday" (11:14, 16–17).

Job is exasperated, and responds with sarcasm: "No doubt you are the people, and wisdom will die with you" (12:2).Their attitudes are cruel: "I am a laughing-stock to my friends . . . Those at ease have contempt for misfortune" (12:4–5). It is so unjust: "The tents of robbers are at peace, and those who provoke God are secure" (12:6). This leads to a speech on the superiority of God and the futility of human pride: "He leads counselors away stripped, and makes fools of judges. . . . He deprives of speech those who are trusted, and takes away the discernment of the elders" (12:17, 20). Leaders are stripped of understanding and stagger around like drunks (12:24–25).

Still, "I desire to argue my case with God" (13:3). He is bringing a legal case. "Listen to the pleadings of my lips" (13:6) uses a noun, *ribôt*, that is "a juridical term."[24] He challenges the friends: "Will you speak falsely for God?" (13:7). Job insists on choosing the testimony of *personal experience* over the dogmas of standardized theology. He *sees* that the wicked often prosper. He will continue to challenge God, although he knows he places his life in danger by doing so: "I will take my flesh in my teeth, and put

23. Vicchio, *Job*, 96; Andersen, *Job*, 169.
24. Pope, *Job*, 98.

my life in my hand. See, he will kill me; I have no hope; but I will defend my ways to his face" (13:14–15). The KJV rendered the latter verse thus: "Though he slay me, yet will I trust in him: but I will maintain mine own ways before him." The important medieval commentator Rashi paraphrased it thus: "Though He slay me . . . I shall not separate myself from Him and shall always trust in Him."[25] It certainly is a very audacious statement, whether it is audaciously trusting or audaciously defiant. I see him expressing both faith and defiance in the same breath. The view that emphasizes trust is supported by what follows, where he affirms that God's righteousness will yield a fair verdict: "This will be my salvation, that the godless shall not come before him . . . I shall be vindicated" (13:16, 18). Again we have the judicial setting, although Job's role is not exactly clear. H. H. Rowley says Job "is equally willing to appear as plaintiff or defendant."[26]

He is asking for God's response. "Then call, and I will answer" (13:22). He believes he will be vindicated. But he does not claim to be completely sinless; he is willing that God "make me know my transgression and my sin" (13:23). Unfortunately, he now wanders into bitter complaining: "Why do you hide your face, and count me as your enemy? . . . You put my feet in the stocks, and watch all my paths" (13:24, 27).

The Afterlife Affirmation in 14:13–18

These pessimistic reflections lead Job to reflect upon the weary fate of all humans: "A mortal, born of woman, few of days and full of trouble, comes up like a flower and withers" (14:1–2). He repeats the gloomy belief about the afterlife: "For there is hope for a tree, if it is cut down, that it will sprout again . . . But mortals die, and are laid low; humans expire, and where are they?" (14:7, 10).

This bleak afterlife concept is the dogma that Job most wants to reject, the notion that everyone descends down into the dust:

25. Vicchio, *Job*, 107.
26. Rowley, "Intellectual Versus Spiritual," 124; Vicchio, *Job*, 109.

"mortals lie down and do not rise again" (14:12). They "live in houses of clay, whose foundation is in the dust" (4:19). Of *all* people, regardless of the kind of life they lived, Job says "They lie down alike in the dust, and the worms cover them" (21:26). This is the traditional Mesopotamian belief, which the Israelites inherited. Sometimes they thought that people lay there in a dim, half-conscious state, eating dust: a wholly gloomy existence. Job is struggling with God on the subject of suffering, and part of that struggle involves his occasional rebellion against this gloomy belief.

However, there may be more afterlife optimism in this passage than appears at first glance. The mention of a tree "sprout[ing] again" may draw upon an Egyptian theme of trees as a source of rest and renewal in the afterlife, even a symbol of the revival of the dying god, Osiris.[27] Later, he again uses tree imagery for his recovery: "with the dew all night on my branches" (29:19).[28] There are Egyptian loan words in 9:26 and 12:21.[29] It may be that the author of Job drew upon a certain optimistic theme in Egyptian religion as an answer to the pessimism of Mesopotamian beliefs, which held sway over Jewish beliefs. So, before Job's depressing words in 14:10–12 is a vivid afterlife image. Then again, *after* those despairing words, is a remarkable expression of afterlife hope.

It seems that Job's own personal experience presses him to make a theological affirmation. He senses that the accepted doctrine of Sheol, a sleepy sameness for everyone (14:12), is inadequate. He states it in *personal* terms, rather than as a doctrine; he prays "O that you would hide me in Sheol . . . until your wrath is past, that you would appoint me a set time, and remember me!" (14:13). Pope says, "Job here gropes toward the idea of an afterlife."[30] When Job asks "If mortals die, will they live again?" (14:14), he is looking for a new answer, rather than the standard (negative) one. It seems only logical that "All the days of my service I would wait until my release should come. You would call, and I would answer

27. Hays, "There Is Hope for a Tree," 44–51, 58–68.
28. Hays, "There Is Hope for a Tree," 65.
29. Boss, *Human Consciousness*, 81.
30. Pope, *Job*, 108. See also Driver, *Book of Job*, xx.

you; you would long for the work of your hands" (14:14–15). Job's personal faith pushes him to this positive outburst.

Newsom agrees that "Job is talking here about resurrection and death"; the "service" of 14:14 is *tsᵉbā*, "as in a labor gang or an army."[31] His release from service, then, is his resurrection, his release from the labor gang of life. By asserting hope here, he is reversing his words of 13:15, where he says "I have no hope."[32] Regarding the "call" and "answer" in 14:15, Andersen says this is "answering the prayer of 13:22 (using exactly the same words)."[33] In these same verbs, Hays sees "mortuary overtones" and "the longing of a god for reunion" from "an Egyptian text from the tomb of the vizier Paser (TT106)."[34]

Upon the basis of his personal hope in God, Job reasons that God would *want to see the work of his hands*, would not want to let that work, that person, go to waste. It is a profoundly important and true religious insight: that nothing good is ever wasted. This relates to "the conviction that no value perishes out of the world. . . . belief in the conservation of value."[35] As a British poet promised: "There shall never be one lost good! What was, shall live as before."[36]

Job goes on to tell God that God's attitude would not always be judgmental, for "then you would not number my steps, you would not keep watch over my sin" (14:16). The realization that God is not judgmentally watching over his sin is a real breakthrough for Job. He is able to confidently assert a belief in God's forgiveness: "my transgression would be sealed up in a bag, and you would cover over my iniquity" (14:17).

The oldest known interpreter of the Hebrew book of Job is its Greek translation, the Septuagint version of Job, which is not

31. Newsom, *Book of Job*, 168. "Hard service" (Janzen, *Job*, 111).

32. Newsom, *Book of Job*, 168.

33. Andersen, *Job*, 186.

34. Hays, "There Is Hope for a Tree," 61. TT refers to the catalog of Theban tombs.

35. Höffding, *Philosophy of Religion*, 6.

36. Browning, "Abt Vogler," *Selected Poems*, 225.

strictly a translation but a translation with interpretive alterations and insertions. The Septuagint version changes the question in 14:14 to a declaration: "If a man dies, he shall live again." Further, the LXX adds words to 42:17: "And it is written that he will rise again with those whom the Lord has raised up."[37] I do think that Job 14 is speaking about the afterlife, although he is unable to confidently sustain this faith throughout the Dialogue. The Septuagint interpreter is so sure of the afterlife understanding that he adds some material to support this interpretation. The Septuagint translator also softens some of the sharper edges in the story. Where the MT says that Job's brothers and sisters "comforted him for all the evil that the Lord had brought upon him" (42:11), the LXX says "all 'the *things* the Lord Yнwн had brought to him.'"[38]

The Jewish medieval commentator Gersonides also sees that, for Job in chapter 14, "resurrection is a possibility."[39] The book of Job is a theological drama, and Job's struggle toward faith in an afterlife is one of the key dramatic breakthroughs in the book. Chapter 14 contains the first expression of afterlife hope in Job. It will be followed by another brief but vivid expression of hope in chapter 19. The book of Job is an adventure in ideas, and these exclamations of belief, rejecting the gloomy afterlife concept, are two of the supreme breakthroughs in the drama, although the Job character seems unable to hold onto this faith. In fact, what immediately follows reverts to the despairing remarks of earlier, saying that as "the waters wear away the stones . . . so you destroy the hope of mortals. You prevail forever against them, and they pass away" (14:19–20).[40]

37. Vicchio, *Job*, 1, 16.
38. Guillaume, "Dismantling," 498.
39. Quoted in Vicchio, *Job*, 15.
40. His afterlife hope is held "only momentarily": Pope, *Job*, lxxvi.

The Debate Resumes

Eliphaz takes his turn, without really responding to what Job just said. This time "he is much less courteous" than in chapters 4–5.[41] Job is a windbag, taught by iniquity (15:2, 5). Maybe Job even dares to claim that he has "listened in the council of God" and possibly limits "wisdom to yourself" (15:8). He has turned against God, and has become "abominable" (15:13, 16). Despite the changed tone, Eliphaz's message is still the same: God punishes evildoers (15:20) and those who are defiant (15:25); "they will live in desolate cities" and "their branch will not be green" (15:28, 32).

Job rejects the words of his "miserable comforters" (16:2). But it is God, finally, who has brought him low: "Surely now God has worn me out . . . he has shriveled me up . . . he has torn me in his wrath, and hated me" (16:7–9). That last verb has the "connotation of bearing a grudge or cherishing animosity."[42] Again, though he complains about God, he also sees God as his future vindicator: "O earth, do not cover my blood; let my outcry find no resting-place. Even now, in fact, my witness is in heaven, and he that vouches for me is on high" (16:18–19). As it is, Job is running out of days: "My spirit is broken, my days are extinct, the grave is ready for me . . . My days are past, my plans are broken off, the desires of my heart [*lvav*]" (17:1, 11). Rowley thinks that Job, in v. 11, is speaking of being near to death.[43] This line of thinking continues: "Where then is my hope? . . . Will it go down to the bars of Sheol?" (17:15–16).[44] Here, as throughout most of the Dialogue, God remains "the far-off object of desire,"[45] according to Jeffrey Boss.

Bildad is offended that he and his friends are "counted as cattle . . . stupid" by Job (18:3). Newsom notes that Job has not called them cattle, but that he *is* attacking "the herd mentality embedded

---

41. Pope, *Job*, 114.

42. Boss, *Human Consciousness*, 93.

43. Rowley, "Intellectual Versus Spiritual," 156; Vicchio, *Job*, 131.

44. Vicchio, *Job*, 133.

45. Boss, *Human Consciousness*, 97.

in" their clichés.[46] Bildad goes on to repeat the familiar argument that it is the wicked who suffer (18:5–8). In fact, "their own schemes throw them down. For they are thrust into a net by their own feet" (18:7–8). Bildad's reference to skin disease seems to be including Job in the company of the wicked: "By disease their skin is consumed, the firstborn of Death consumes their limbs" (18:13).[47] Everyone sees the downfall of the wicked: "they are thrust from light into darkness, and driven out of the world" (18:18).

The Redeemer in 19:25

Job rebukes his "friends" for tormenting him (19:2). He allows that he may have erred (19:4), but still "you magnify yourselves against me" (19:5). Again he turns his attention to God, who "has stripped my glory" and "kindled his wrath against me" (19:9, 11). His friends abhor him, "even young children despise me," and "I have escaped by the skin of my teeth" (19:18–20). The meaning of "skin of my teeth" is unclear, but it seems to indicate a narrow escape from death.[48]

However, a certain energy has been building up in Job and it now bursts out in an expression of faith: "O that my words were written down! O that they were inscribed in a book! O that with an iron pen and with lead they were engraved on a rock forever! For I know that my Redeemer lives, and that at the last he will stand upon the earth; and after my skin has been thus destroyed, then in my flesh I shall see God" (19:23–26). Job 19:26 has suffered some textual damage; "in my flesh" could be "without my flesh," according to NRSV's marginal alternative. Matthew Suriano translates it as "without my flesh."[49] Amy Erickson points out "where 'in flesh' is intended, it is clearly expressed with the preposition ב" b-,

---

46. Newsom, *Book of Job*, 175; and see Vicchio, *Job*, 135.

47. On Death, "the Ravenous One," in vv. 12–13, see Pope, *Job*, 132, 135.

48. Pope, *Job*, 143.

49. Suriano, "Job's Kinsman-Redeemer," 56.

instead of מִן *min*, which indicates separation.[50] Further, "after my skin has been thus destroyed" could more appropriately be "after this has struck off my very skin," meaning after his affliction or his condition has struck off the skin.[51]

As in chapter 14, Job is moved by the inward pressure of faith to resist the external pressure of conventional belief. This is what makes Job a great book: the inward struggle for truth, the outward drama of conflicting religious views, and the fact that the character Job is allowed to follow his own deepest instincts, and so to burst out with new insights, even if he cannot sustain them throughout his speeches.

How true to life this is! How often must the expression of religious truth be an outburst of aspiration and an act of nonconformity! And how difficult it sometimes is for the nonconformist to hold fast to the new truth, and not to lose heart. Jesus took note of this challenge, and so "Jesus told them a parable about their need to pray always and not to lose heart" (Luke 18:1). Job sometimes rallies, and sometimes loses heart.

To understand the passage in Job 19, it is necessary to do some background research. This discloses that the passage is set within the environment of burial rites. The descriptions of his flesh decaying, "after my skin is struck off" and "my kidneys shrivel within my bosom" (19:26–27, Suriano's translation), are images of death.[52] Job's desire that his words were engraved in stone (19:23–24) calls to mind the traditional recording of an epitaph.[53] The *goel* in v. 25 is the kinsman-redeemer, who performs the necessary rites and inscribes an epitaph.[54]

The literal meaning is that the redeemer speaks in Job's defense, over his dead body, but the metaphorical actor appears to be someone (likely God) speaking for Job and letting Job see him, even after his flesh has been destroyed. It seems to be an

50. Erickson, "Without My Flesh," 308.

51. Boss, *Human Consciousness*, 105.

52. Suriano, "Job's Kinsman-Redeemer," 56.

53. Suriano, "Job's Kinsman-Redeemer," 59.

54. Suriano, "Job's Kinsman-Redeemer," 59.

anticipation of an afterlife where Job will see his redeemer, God. This would be consistent with Job's declaration that "my witness is in heaven, and he that vouches for me is on high" (16:19). Vicchio recalls Job calling for "a *mokiah*, or 'arbiter'" in 9:33.[55] It also seems to be partially echoed later, when Elihu envisions "an angel, a mediator, one of a thousand," who rescues a person from "going down into the Pit'" (33:23–24), although *that* rescuing takes place in *this* lifetime, and it is an angel who pulls a person back from the pit of death.

Suriano stays close to a literal reading, asserting that what is at stake is an honorable versus a dishonorable death. "It is Job's kinsman-redeemer, through the performance of his duties, who will act against this threat and effectively preserve Job's name."[56] But I think Suriano is underestimating the metaphorical force of this passage. If postmortem honor is all that is at stake, it is hard to account for the *live* encounter embraced in the saying "I shall see God" (19:26). The literal referent is clearly a kinsman-redeemer, and he may indeed be, as Suriano insists, functioning in the role of preserving the memory of the deceased Job, but the author uses this metaphorically. It is *God* who will preserve Job himself, and not just his memory. Job will be alive to *see* God, stated in v. 26[57] and repeated in v. 27 ("whom I shall see on my side, and my eyes shall behold, and not another"). It is an afterlife vision, in contrast to the gloomy half-awake sleep of Mesopotamian imagining. Job envisions a fully awake state where he is able to see God.

Vicchio also wants to stick with a literal understanding. "The *Goel* is to be a human being . . . Nowhere else in the Hebrew Bible is the word *Goel* used to describe anyone other than a person who seeks revenge for some wrong done to a member of his family or clan," and he then speaks approvingly of David Clines's notion that the *Goel* may be Job himself.[58]

55. Vicchio, *Job*, 147.

56. Suriano, "Job's Kinsman-Redeemer," 65.

57. Noted by Pope, *Job*, 146.

58. Vicchio, *Job*, 147; "his 'cry' is personified as witness, advocate, and spokesman . . . He has to be his own *gōēl*" (Clines, *Job 1–20*, 459).

But I think the metaphor of God as *Goel* works perfectly well. Further, God as *Goel* is an image that occurs *numerous* times in the Bible, being a main theme of Second Isaiah (Pss 19:14; 78:35; Prov 23:11; Isa 41:14; 43:14; 48:17; 49:7; 54:5). Job 19:25 is a dramatic high point in the tale, and expresses one of Job's momentary assertions of faith. However, Job is unable to remain at the height where he makes the affirmation. It is a flash of faith that quickly fades. "The flashes are always followed by the most profound darkness. The old patriarchal conception returns and presses upon him with its whole weight."[59]

Dhorme translates *Goel* as "vindicator," looking at the role the term plays in Proverbs 23:10–11 and Psalm 119:154.[60] Most Christian interpreters, from the patristic period to the eighteenth century, believed the *Goel* was a prophecy of Christ.[61] I would consider that to be anachronistic, and a projecting of one's theology onto the text. But it does seem clear throughout that Job hopes to be vindicated by God, and it seems that here, as in 14:14–15, he hopes God will raise him up and commune with him after his death. "There should be no doubt that the *Redeemer* is *God*."[62]

The Hebrew text of Job 19:25b–27 appears to be "quite corrupted," and has caused nightmares for translators.[63] "My redeemer lives" in 19:25 is clear, but what is happening with the flesh is less clear. As we saw above, the phrase translated "in my flesh" in 19:26 by NRSV and NIV is better translated "without my flesh."[64] It has even been proposed to translate it "refleshed by him," meaning "the creation of a new body for the afterlife."[65] Gerald Janzen

---

59. Renan, "Cry of the Soul," 120.

60. Dhorme, *Commentary*, 283.

61. Among others: Ephrem the Syrian, John Chrysostom, Thomas Aquinas, Jerome, John Wesley; Vicchio, *Job*, 148–49.

62. Andersen, *Job*, 209.

63. Vicchio, *Job*, 147–48; "the text having suffered irreparable damage"; Pope, *Job*, lxxvi.

64. Erickson, "Without My Flesh," 308; Vicchio, *Job*, 152.

65. Dahood, *Psalms II*, second note on Ps lxxiii 26; quoted in Pope, *Job*, 147. Dahood amends *mibbĕśārî* to the Pu'al participle *mĕbuśśārî* with a third person suffix.

writes of "Job as seeing God from a newly embodied state."[66] The point is that "Job's hope reaches toward a restored vision of God."[67]

Job's heroic struggle is a part of what we see throughout the Old Testament, and his "pious protest" is not uncommon: "Job joins the heroes of Israelite faith, Abraham, Jacob, Moses, the psalmists, and prophets, in demanding that God make things right. They struggle with God, but never let him go, because of their faith in his justice, goodness, and power."[68] "It is out of Job's unfaltering conviction of his innocence that his great declaration of belief in a future life in xix.25ff. springs."[69] The hard questions and the partial answers are all part of "the good fight of the faith" (1 Tim 6:12).

Back and Forth

Zophar is impatient with Job's words, and implies that they are "the exulting of the wicked" (20:5). There is an intriguing line: "His children must make amends to the poor; his own hands must give back his wealth" (20:10 NIV). This seems to imply that Job has exploited the poor, and he and his children will have to pay them back.[70] A similar pronouncement is this: "They will give back the fruit of their toil . . . for they have crushed and abandoned the poor" (20:18–19). The fact that the prose Prologue had all his children being killed is just another example of the disconnect between the Prologue and the Dialogue. Nor does the Prologue give any hint that Job or his family oppressed anyone.

Zophar is very dogmatic and confident that the wicked are always punished. They will be made sick or poisoned (20:14–16); "they knew no quiet" and "the possessions of their house will be carried away" (20:20, 28). Without saying so directly, Zophar

66. Janzen, *Job*, 144.

67. Janzen, *Job*, 145.

68. Kynes and Kynes, *Wrestling with Job*, 152.

69. Driver, *Book of Job*, xx.

70. Vicchio, *Job*, 155.

implies that Job is wicked and is suffering justly. He doesn't even notice Job's expression of hope for an afterlife.

Job's reply takes up again the issue of the wicked prospering (21:7–20), in contrast with Zophar's stubborn insistence that the wicked do *not* prosper. Job says "How often is the lamp of the wicked put out? How often does calamity come upon them?" (21:17), implying "not often enough." Job wonders "who repays them for what they have done?" (21:31). The wicked die peacefully and are respected (21:13, 32). Further, he challenges the notion that God will punish the children of evildoers (21:19). He wishes "let their own eyes see their destruction" (21:20), thus agreeing with Jeremiah's and Ezekiel's (Jer 31:29–30; Ezek 18:1–4) rejection of the common idea that God punishes "subsequent generations for the sin of the father," such as is found in Exodus 20:5; Deuteronomy 5:9; and Lamentations 5:7.[71] Jeremiah and Job agree with Ezekiel that "it is only the person who sins who" should have to pay for that sin (Ezek 18:4). Unfortunately, the wicked *do* get to live long and prosperous lives (Job 21:30–31), and are honored after death (21:32). Zophar's views, Job says, are "empty nothings"[72] and "falsehood" (21:34).

Eliphaz does not reply to any of these points. In fact, many of the speeches in the book do not reply directly to the preceding speech. Eliphaz asks what does a mortal even matter: "Can a mortal be of use to God? Can even the wisest be of service to him? Is it any pleasure to the Almighty if you are righteous?" (22:2–3). However, he insists, Job is *not* righteous: "Is not your wickedness great? There is no end to your iniquities" (22:5). In direct contradiction to the narrator's and Yahweh's statements (1:2, 8) and to Job's claim of innocence (10:7; 9:21), Eliphaz asserts that Job "withheld bread from the hungry . . . and the arms of the orphans you have crushed" (22:7, 9). Eliphaz makes false claims, saying that Job had said that God does not know or see (22:13–14). Eliphaz sees Job as wicked (22:15), and warns that the wicked are "snatched away

---

71. Vicchio, *Job*, 163.

72. Using the same word, *hebel*, as Ecclesiastes uses for "vanity" (Andersen, *Job*, 217).

before their time," that "the righteous see it and are glad; the innocent laugh them to scorn" (22:16, 19). The judgmentalism of the friends seems to be getting more intense. Implying that Job has turned away from God, Eliphaz tells him to "return to the Almighty . . . for he saves the humble" (22:23, 29). A brief glimpse of God's mercy is had at the end of this speech: "He will deliver even those who are guilty" (22:30), but it is hardly merciful to be labeling Job as guilty.

Job's response ignores most of what Eliphaz has alleged, but focuses on his desire to find God (23:3), and lay out his case (*riyb*) (23:4); he uses several words that would fit in a court of law.[73] Regarding v. 3, Rowley says "It is the chief distinction between Job and his friends that he desires to meet God and they do not . . . If only God would give him a chance to understand why he was suffering, he would be satisfied."[74] Job asserts that God "would give heed to me. There an upright person could reason with him, and I should be acquitted" (23:6–7). However, his confidence starts to flag again: he looks for God and cannot find him (23:8–9). But then he reasserts confidence: God knows his way, will test him, and he will come out like gold (23:10). Job has "not departed from the commandment" but God "will complete what he appoints for me" (23:12, 14). It's hard to know whether this is confidence or sad resignation. What he says next is that he is afraid (23:15–16). The tenth-century rabbinic interpreter Saadiah Gaon says "Job interprets God's silence as avoidance of the confrontation which he seeks . . . God's silence is a display of arbitrariness of His Power, as Job interprets it."[75]

Job resumes his complaint about the wicked, and notes how the poor and needy suffer (24:2–11). Here he takes up the cause of the poor: "There are those who snatch the orphan child from the breast, and take as a pledge the infant of the poor" (24:9). He is outraged that God does not intervene: "The throat of the wounded cries for help; yet God pays no attention to their prayer" (24:12).

73. Vicchio, *Job*, 173.

74. Rowley, "Intellectual Versus Spiritual," 200; quoted in Vicchio, *Job*, 173.

75. Saadiah, *Book of Theodicy*, 109; quoted in Vicchio, *Job*, 174.

He goes on to narrate the evil that the wicked do, committing murder and adultery (24:14–15), and yet those who "harm the childless woman, and do no good to the widow" (24:21) do not suffer; "God prolongs the[ir] life . . . He gives them security, and they are supported" (24:22–23). But even *their* time on earth is short: "They are exalted a little while, and then are gone; they wither and fade like the mallow" (24:24).

Summarizing the book to this point, Boss says that Job has come to certain realizations. "He realizes that he is of value to God . . . He comes to the knowledge that he will indeed encounter God, his vindicator." He has also become aware that not only he, but others suffer innocently as well.[76] Yet, "God is still the far-off object of desire" for Job.[77]

Bildad does not respond to Job's points, but asks "How then can a mortal be righteous before God?" (25:4). A human is "a maggot . . . a worm" (25:6). Bildad's reply is so short, and some of the material in the following chapters fits so well with Bildad's argument, that scholars such as S. Viccio, W. B. Stevenson, and M. Pope have concluded that 26:5–14 was originally part of Bildad's speech.[78] That passage is mostly a naturalistic and mythic description of God's power: "the pillars of heaven tremble . . . But the thunder of his power who can understand?" (26:11, 14). There are some archaic terms, such as *Rephaim* in 26:5[79] (translated "the shades" in NRSV[80]) and *Abaddon* in 26:6, sometimes translated as "Destruction,"[81] but left untranslated in NRSV. Verse 13 has the "fleeing serpent," which some have thought is equivalent to Leviathan.[82]

---

76. Boss, *Human Consciousness*, 128.

77. Boss, *Human Consciousness*, 129.

78. Vicchio, *Job*, 184; Pope, *Job*, 180.

79. Vicchio, *Job*, 185.

80. Also translated as "shades" in Isaiah 26:14, and as "the dead" in Proverbs 21:16; Isaiah 26:19. In other texts (Gen 14:5; Deut 2:11, 20; 3:11), the Rephaim are an extinct race of giants (Pope, *Job*, 183).

81. Vicchio, *Job*, 186, 193. Pope translates it as "Perdition," and notes that the word is transliterated into Greek in Rev 9:11 (Pope, *Job*, 183).

82. Vicchio, *Job*, 186.

Job's reply to Bildad is sarcastic: "How you have counseled one who has no wisdom, and given much good advice!" (26:3). He returns to his complaint that God has "taken away my right," even though he did "not speak falsehood" (27:2, 4). An interesting response, although not entirely accurate, is this: "The poet raises Job to the bleak summit of righteousness bereft of hope, bereft of faith in divine justice."[83] This is not wholly accurate because Job is still affirming God's justice in these final parts of his speaking (27:8, 13; 31:6). Yet he will maintain his innocence: "as long as my breath is in me and the spirit of God is in my nostrils, my lips will not speak falsehood . . . until I die I will not put away my integrity from me" (27:3–5). The appeal to the spirit within (27:3) anticipates what Elihu will say later about his being empowered by the spirit (32:8; 33:4). Some of the material in this chapter again sounds like the friends, recounting how God punishes the wicked: "If their children are multiplied, it is for the sword . . . They go to bed with wealth, but will do so no more; they open their eyes, and it is gone" (27:14, 19). Edwin Good thinks 27:7–10, 13–23 are "perhaps to be assigned to Zophar."[84] They would then be part of the missing third speech of Zophar.

Andersen disagrees with these attempts to assign some of these passages to Bildad or Zophar. The mythic imagery of 26:5–14 anticipates Yahweh's similar imagery in chapters 38–39, although it *does* seem that Job has momentarily set aside the issue of the suffering of the just,[85] and switched to affirming the power of God, and his judgment of the wicked. He has become confident in refuting the three friends' judgment of him. We may even have, in 27:7–23, a prolonged curse against the friends.[86]

---

83. Kaufmann, "Job the Righteous Man," 67.

84. Good, *Irony*, 199.

85. Andersen, *Job*, 233.

86. Andersen, *Job*, 237.

The Hymnic Chapter 28

Then comes a stand-alone chapter that has long been recognized as out of place. Chapter 28 is a soliloquy on wisdom. It does not carry any of the complaints or claims that the character Job makes throughout the drama; it sounds more consistent with the views of Yahweh in the final chapters. Like the material in 26:5–14, it contains much naturalistic and mythic content. In v. 22, Abaddon is mentioned again and is personified.[87] Abaddon and Death have heard a rumor of wisdom, but only God knows the way to it (28:22–24). The last verse (28) is one of only two places in Job where the divine name Yahweh seems to be indicated, although here it uses the euphemism, *Adonai*, and makes a very Proverbs-sounding statement: "the fear of the Lord, that is wisdom" (28:28; cf. Prov 4:7; 9:10; also see Sir 1:14). Many editors omit this verse,[88] but it seems unnecessary to delete this important conclusion from the chapter. The message of the chapter is that wisdom resides with God: "God understands the way to it" (28:23), but "it is hidden from the eyes of all living" (28:21).

Andersen notes that chapter 28 does not fit well with Job's speech. "Its calm and detached mood contrasts with the frenzy of Job's closing speeches, and it expresses a contentment with the inscrutability of the ways of God . . . which Job has not yet attained."[89] However, Andersen strongly resists all suggestions of different authorship for various parts of the book, and he opines that chapter 28 is "a comment by the author," and not by the character, Job.[90] Its tone is too calm to be a displaced speech by any of the characters, "for everyone has lost his temper at the end of the discussion."[91]

---

87. Vicchio, *Job*, 193.

88. Vicchio, *Job*, 193; Pope, *Job*, 206.

89. Andersen, *Job*, 55.

90. Andersen, *Job*, 55.

91. Andersen, *Job*, 241.

The Final Chapters of the Debate

Job resumes his self-defense in chapter 29. First he laments his lost bliss: "when the friendship of God was upon my tent; when the Almighty was still with me, when my children were around me" (29:4–5). He was good to people: "I delivered the poor . . . the orphan" and "caused the widow's heart to sing for joy" (29:12–13). He "championed the cause of the stranger" and "broke the fangs of the unrighteous" (29:16–17). This makes it all the harder to endure how "now they make sport of me" (30:1). The present-tense emphasis continues: "now they mock me in song . . . now my soul is poured out within me" (30:9, 16). His bones are in pain, he has been cast into the mire (30:17, 19). In the only passage in the chapter where he again addresses God directly, he says God is the ultimate source of the mistreatment: "You have turned cruel to me; with the might of your hand you persecute me" (30:21; re-calling the complaint of 16:9, "he has torn me in his wrath, and hated me"). Edwin Good notes that Job directly addresses God in 17:3–4, but not again until the passage in 30:20–23. Good says the reduction in direct address is because Job has lost hope that he will get a fair hearing.[92] It certainly is a sad narrative, especially when contrasted with the happy life described in chapter 29.

Job feels unjustly treated: "Did I not weep for those whose day was hard? Was not my soul grieved for the poor? But when I looked for good, evil came, and when I waited for light, dark-ness came" (30:25–26). He suffers some kind of skin disease: "My skin turns black and falls from me, and my bones burn with heat" (30:30).

In chapter 31 he returns to reviewing the past, claiming he has not "walked with falsehood" (31:5), and he trusts that, by God, he is "weighed in a just balance" (31:6). Hays sees an echo of Egyp-tian religious thinking in the image of a balance for the soul.[93] If Job has transgressed in any way, then may another eat what he has sown (31:7–8), using language similar to Deuteronomy 28:30 and

92. Good, *Irony*, 232.
93. Hays, "There Is Hope for a Tree," 57.

Isaiah 65:22.[94] It is a self-curse. Another self-imprecation follows. If he has been "enticed by a woman . . . then let my wife grind for another . . . For that would be a heinous crime" (31:9–11). The word translated "heinous crime" is *zimmāh*, which would better be translated "licentiousness"[95] or "lewdness."[96] In 31:13–15 he claims not to have ignored the claims of "my male or female slaves," not placing one gender above the other. Both have rights. In fact, "Did not he who made me in the womb make them?" (31:15). Nor has he withheld anything from the poor, the widow, or the orphan (31:16–18). If he has ever raised his hand against an orphan, then, "let my shoulder blade fall from my shoulder" (v. 22). God is their protector, and retaliation would follow (v. 23).

Verses 26–28 might indicate that he did not participate in pagan worship, did not kiss idols.[97] The chapter continues with the logic that if he has mistreated anyone, let him be punished. He has not been stingy, greedy, vengeful, or inhospitable (31:16, 24, 29, 32). He seems to admit to "transgressions," but has not hidden them (31:33). He is willing to give "an account of all my steps" (31:37). He is still asking for a hearing. And this is where he ends: "The words of Job are ended" (31:40).

Margulies argues that the poetic Dialogue was originally an independent and complete work. He argues for an "overwhelming sense that Job won the debate in chaps. 29–31."[98] Job's confidence in arguing with God has grown from tentativeness in chapter 9 to boldness in chapter 13 to his demandingness in the final chapters.[99] Margulies sees the Dialogue ending in chapter 31 with no resolution and no answer from God. It may be, though, that Job has "found *in his reader* the empathy and recognition he demanded of God in vain."[100] The redactor who added the theophany of chap-

94. Vicchio, *Job*, 206.
95. Pope, *Job*, 231–32.
96. Boss, *Human Consciousness*, 153.
97. Pope, *Job*, 235; Vicchio, *Job*, 209.
98. Margulies, "Oh That One," 604.
99. Margulies, "Oh That One," 600.
100. Margulies, "Oh That One," 602.

ters 38–42 wants to offer a partial rebuttal to Job's complaints and counteract "the overwhelming sense that Job won the debate in chaps. 29–31."[101]

I find it hard to believe that an author simply ended the work where we find the end of chapter 31, with no resolution of any kind. Margulies thinks it ends with Job winning the debate with God, but it seems more likely to me that the framework was already there, and the Dialogue was written with an awareness of the theophany that would follow. But first we have another viewpoint to consider.

The target of most of the debate chapters is providence theology, the view that sickness and death are consequences of sin, and that the just are always rewarded with health and prosperity. This was a common belief in the ancient world, and an especially intense belief in wisdom literature, as seen in the words of the three friends of Job, in Proverbs,[102] and in the wisdom literature of Egypt. It is quite a conformist and conservative theology. Job is the character who gets beyond conformity and seeks truth courageously, but he also displays some of the flaws of people who get beyond conformity: restlessness, moodiness, isolation, feelings of being persecuted.

Providence theology is not very satisfying, morally or intellectually. In fact, even some Proverbs struggle against the view that righteousness is unfailingly rewarded in this lifetime: Some Proverbs advocate for the poor, who can, in fact, be made to suffer unjustly (14:31; 19:17).[103] But the chief critic of providence theology is Job.

ELIHU'S INTERVENTION

Responses to Elihu

Elihu is the speaker who interrupts the Dialogue in Job with a long speech (chaps. 32 to 37). While the other characters seem to have

---

101. Margulies, "Oh That One," 604.

102. Prov 10:3; 12:2; 16:5; 22:4, 8–9, for instance.

103. Kynes and Kynes, *Wrestling with Job*, 76.

Edomite names, Elihu's name and ancestry seem definitely Judean, and, in fact, his name may be a variant spelling of Elijah.[104] Elihu seems, in most ways, to be beyond the conformity/nonconformity dichotomy. He does not make a virtue out of either conformity or nonconformity. I see Elihu in this way because I focus on the intellectual and theological principles that he emphasizes. If I handled him only *dramatically* or *narratively*, I would have to come to very different conclusions, as many scholars have done. Elihu distracts from the central drama with a somewhat pompous speech, confidently declaring "the uprightness of my heart" (33:3). Unhappy with Elihu's attitude, many scholars actually despise him, calling him a "bigot," a "bore,"[105] "unintelligible."[106] He "does not understand himself."[107] Because of Elihu's remark "My heart is indeed like wine that has no vent; like new wineskins, it is ready to burst" (32:19), Sutherland opines, "Elihu's words are but flatulence or defecation."[108] Generally, these scholars overlook the actual theology imparted by this character.[109] Far more helpful is the astute analysis of Carol Newsom, who acknowledges that Elihu "intrudes into an intense moment" at the end of the cycles of speeches and offers "tendentious interpretations,"[110] but who also insists that "Elihu's arguments differ significantly from those of the friends" of Job, and that he brings an important focus on "ideas."[111]

Newsom's balanced approach is a welcome relief from the many pious and judgmental remarks of scholars who are upset by Elihu's pious and judgmental remarks! Too many scholars are so incensed by the preachiness of Elihu that they pay little attention

104. Gordis, *Book of God*, 115.

105. J. B. Curtis and E. Good, respectively, quoted in Newsom, "Job," 564.

106. Good, *In Turns of Tempest*, 329.

107. Janzen, *Job*, 220.

108. Sutherland, *Putting God on Trial*, Kindle loc. 899–903.

109. Others give no consideration to Elihu at all. Brueggemann and Linafelt dismiss him in two sentences (Brueggemann and Linafelt, *Introduction to the Old Testament*, 331).

110. Newsom, "Job," 564–65.

111. Newsom, "Job," 563–64; a similar point is made by Clines, *Job 21–37*, 742–43.

to what he actually preaches. He puts an emphasis on mercy not found elsewhere in the book. God's rescuing mercy is stressed, especially near the beginning of Elihu's monologue: "God indeed does all these things, twice, three times, with mortals, to bring back their souls from the Pit" (33:29–30).

Elihu does indeed assert the superiority of his own views, and tries to exert a controlling influence on the discussion. This is presumptuous, but not fatal. We need to examine the content of Elihu's teaching, and not be distracted by his youthful bravado. His teachings bespeak a spiritual and philosophic versatility not encountered in the self-righteous "friends," the struggling Job, or the defensive and imperious Yahweh.

Some people are put off by Elihu's urgency, perhaps the same way they are put off by door-to-door evangelists, but let us grant this young man his ten minutes. What if a real prophet has knocked on our door? Wouldn't we expect a young evangelist to give a somewhat overly confident summary of God's ways? That does not mean he is devoid of truth. We may need to season his truth with the salt of our own experience, but we should not miss out on the nourishment he offers.

It may be that his well-scrubbed young face, his simple and optimistic message, his lack of doubts, are more than we jaded intellectuals can tolerate. But are we as true to *our* age and experience as he is to his? Can we get equally lively results from our own experience and insight?

Elihu's Theology

It seems that Elihu is first of all a *reader* of (an earlier version of) Job, and *then* a writer who inserts himself into the Dialogue.[112] Elihu gives us our first glimpse of an engaged reader's response to the text. As soon as Elihu is done, the story picks up where it left off without a hint that any of the other characters are even aware of Elihu's existence. When the Lord tells Eliphaz that his wrath

112. Newsom calls him a "dissatisfied reader" of Job (Newsom, *Book of Job*, 200).

is kindled against him "and against your two friends" (42:7), no notice is taken of Elihu.

Elihu charges into the story with his own views. He will not support the friends' (conformist) view that those who suffer must deserve it, nor will he support Job's (nonconformist) suggestion that God is unjust when he allows the wicked to prosper and the innocent to suffer. It is the very *tendency* to criticize God that Elihu cannot stand. He objects to ideas that impugn the character of God in any way. His theology is entirely based on the just and gracious character of God. I think it likely that Elihu was a preacher. He is very concerned with what is said about God. He is not inclined to be patient with complaints that arise out of personal experience. He is very concerned that anything said about God should be truthful.

Elihu has a few main answers to which he returns through the course of his speech. They are all rejoinders to Job's outbursts. I list them in the order of their first occurrence, but I include all the occurrences of each theme:

1. God's spirit gives life and understanding—32:8, 18; 33:4; 34:14–15—and so

2. Job accuses God unjustly—33:8–12; 34:5–9, 34–37; 35:2, 16—because:

    a. God *does* answer people—33:13–16, 23–28; 35:13–14 (but not the wicked: 35:12);

    b. He rescues people from pride and death—33:17–25; 36:8–9;

    c. He forgives, restores, and gives joy—33:26–30; 36:6;

    d. People can learn wisdom—33:33; 34:4; can choose rightly—33:27; 34:32.

3. Do not ever think it is useless to be in accord with God—34:9; 35:3—because:

    a. God is never unjust; he requites the just and the unjust man; he does not avert his eyes—34:10–30; 35:13–15; 36:3–9, 15; 37:23;

b. He afflicts in order to instruct and rescue—33:19, 23–28; 34:31–32; 36:8–15, 22; 37:13;

c. He hears the afflicted and gives them their right—34:28; 36:6, 15;

d. You cannot hurt God—35:4–11.

4. God is powerful, unfathomable—36:22—37:23—and just (37:23).

Almost all of these are answers to Job's feeling that God does not answer his pleas and that it is useless to seek to be right with God, since he afflicts the just as well as the unjust. But God *does* answer human entreaty with dreams and visions, restoration and rescue, Elihu argues in chapter 33. One should never despair and think that it is useless to be in accord with God, who is *always* just (the message of chapter 34), unflappable and ready to do justice (chapter 35). He gives the afflicted their right; and if he afflicts, it is in order to "reveal" to men the nature of their deeds (chapter 36). We cannot fathom his ways or his powers, but the wise man stands in awe of God, knowing that he does not torment the just (chapter 37). But let us return to Elihu's first point, four times reiterated (32:8, 18; 33:4; and 34:14–15):

God's Spirit gives life and understanding (chapter 32)

This thoroughly biblical doctrine is Elihu's starting point. His remarks in chapter 32 are largely designed to argue for his right to assert the truth. At the only two places where he utters the *content* of that truth (vv. 8 and 18), he says that human understanding comes from the indwelling spirit of God. This is the first and fundamental teaching of Elihu—"truly it is the spirit in a mortal, the breath of the Almighty, that makes for understanding" (32:8), and it is this spirit that *moves* Elihu to speak: "the spirit within me compels me . . . The breath of the Almighty gives me life" (32:18; 33:4b NIV). *This*, and not his age or his status, is his qualification for speaking. The fact that "the breath of the Almighty" is parallel

43

to "spirit of God" in 32:8 highlights "the insight that the human spirit receives from the Spirit of God."[113]

Already we have a truth (God's spirit gives life and understanding) that is barely even considered by any of the other characters, although Job had mentioned the spirit of God in his nostrils (27:3). For Elihu, this inward spirit is a magnet guiding persons toward God. It cannot be left out of the discussion, he insists.

This spirit is central to Elihu's concept of God. Elihu says that the spirit of God is his creator and sustainer (33:4); if God withdrew his spirit, "all flesh would perish together" (34:14–15). Elihu teaches a simple but profound pneumatology: God's spirit is the source of human life *and* wisdom, it commands attention and it imparts understanding.

As we listen to Elihu's claims, we may think that he is overeager, even bombastic (as when he says "For I do not know how to flatter" 32:22), but we should notice the intensity of his awareness of the reality of God; his very *breath* derives from God's breath, he breathes in God's spirit. Of course, in Hebrew, רוּחַ *ruach* means both "breath" and "spirit," but Elihu is remarkable in showing an intensely personal awareness of being filled by God's breath or spirit.

The responsiveness of God (chapter 33)

Elihu reasons upon a basis of confidence in the just and gracious character of God. Elihu seems to be aware that he comes on strong; he tries to reassure Job that "my pressure will not be heavy on you" (33:7). He offers very little of theodicy, but very much of salvation. His advice to Job is to drop the theodicy problem and accept the mercy solution. What disturbs him is Job's nonconformist contending against God (33:13), but he does *not* defend the friends' conformist viewpoint, for "there was in fact no one that confuted Job" (32:12). The friends insist on Job's guilt, while "Job reasons from his innocence to God's injustice."[114] Elihu rejects both positions.

---

113. Hartley, *Book of Job*, 434.

114. Kynes and Kynes, *Wrestling with Job*, 170.

Elihu is focused on truth. He repeats the point about the spirit when he says, "The spirit of God has made me, and the breath of the Almighty gives me life" (33:4). This is why he will speak "sincerely" (33:3). He cannot tolerate the insinuation that God does not answer (33:13) or that God has taken away Job's right (34:5). Job's accusation that God treats him as an enemy even though he is innocent (10:3–7; 13:24–27) is unjust, says Elihu in 33:12, as is the notion that God does not answer him (33:13, responding to 19:7 and 30:20). On the contrary, "God speaks in one way, and in two, though people do not perceive it. In a dream, in a vision of the night, when deep sleep falls on mortals, while they slumber on their beds, then he opens their ears, and terrifies them with warnings" (33:14–16). God's purpose in doing this is correctional: "that he may turn them aside from their deeds, and keep them from pride, to spare their souls from the Pit, their lives from traversing the River" (33:17–18). Everything Elihu says about God is constructive and useful in preaching. Elihu finds it necessary to defend God against criticism.

God sends instructional dreams and visions as warnings against pride (cf. 36:10, where "He opens their ears to instruction"). He chastens people with pain (33:19), until their bones stick out and they are nearly dead (vv. 21–22), then he rescues them, at least if there is an angel to advocate for the person. "If there should be for one of them an angel, a mediator [*mēliṣ*], one of a thousand, one who declares a person upright . . . and says, 'Deliver him from going down into the Pit; I have found a ransom' . . . then he prays to God, and is accepted by him, he comes into his presence with joy, and God repays him for his righteousness" (33:23–24, 26). Then God "let[s] his flesh become fresh with youth" (v. 25, anticipating the restoration that God will give at the end of the book). God's angel is "gracious" (v. 24). The idea of an angel helping a person is also found in Psalm 91:11–12 and Matthew 18:10. Eliphaz had seemingly hinted at this ("To which of the holy ones will you turn?" 5:1), but the context suggests Eliphaz doubts the concept, as his next remarks are on what happens to fools (5:2–5). Eliphaz had also mentioned a frightening night vision he had (4:12–16), but his only lesson from that vision was the untrustworthiness of mortals (4:17–21). But for Elihu, the "nightly dreams could be read as God's daily message of reproof."[115]

Elihu does not doubt the concept of angelic help. However, he is not interested in the question of the injustice of suffering, but only in the truth of God's merciful intervention to save people, including reaching them *through* their suffering. He is answering a different question than the one that Job is asking. Neither Job nor the friends have anything to say about God making extraordinary efforts to save people, to rescue them from the brink of disaster, but that is precisely what Elihu is on fire to proclaim: God sets out "to spare their souls" (33:18). Elihu is upset that the religious drama he is reading has ignored the question of God's active mercy. Elihu burns with enthusiasm to proclaim the spiritual reality of God's efforts to reach, teach, and instruct people.

The saving interest of God is not unique to Elihu's teachings. What *is* unique (within the book of Job, at least) is his insistence that God is full of mercy, always seeking to reach people, speaking in different ways, "though people do not perceive it" (33:14). Elihu sees God as wholly focused on saving people (33:18, 24). Elihu may accept the common view that death is punishment, but what he emphasizes is God's energetic quest to save people. Sickness also is a way for God to reach people (33:19).

Even when a person is on the brink of death, there may be "an angel, a mediator" to declare him "upright" (33:23) and rescue him from the Pit by providing a ransom (*kofer*) for him (33:24). In the family-centered life of the ancient world, most people would have expected a relative to ransom a person who was in a difficult spot, nor was money the only kind of ransom.[116] Elihu's point is the active protection given by God, actually by an angel of God's, who intervenes for a person.

For Elihu, God accepts a repentant person's prayer (which suggests God's attitude is the same as the angel's): "then he will pray to God, and He will accept him, so that he may see His face with

---

115. Fishbane, "Book of Job," 96.
116. Hartley, *Book of Job*, 446.

joy, and he will restore His righteousness to that person" (33:26 NASB). "Seeing God's face" is the preferred translation (HCSB; NASB; NIV; NCV; NABRE; KJV). NRSV has "comes into his presence." Following this glorious experience, "that person sings to others and says, 'I sinned, and perverted what was right, and it was not paid back to me. He has redeemed my soul from going down to the Pit'" (vv. 27–28 NRSV, perhaps an autobiographical insight of the author?). It is an extraordinary experience, where "God accepts him as an upright and blameless person."[117]

Elihu gives God the credit. God is the one who redeems (v. 28), who forgives those who admit they have sinned, and he does this repeatedly: "God indeed does all these things, twice, three times, with mortals, to bring back their souls from the Pit, so that they may see the light of life" (33:29–30).

Apparently, the rescued person needs to admit that he *did* do wrong. Elihu seems to oppose—*on principle*, more than on specific knowledge of Job's actions—any claim of utter innocence. This, then, is a theological crux. Ready willingness to admit that one has "perverted what was right" (v. 27) is essential to being healed. Whether or not an advocating angel is also essential is unclear; angels are not mentioned again, but repentance and prayerfulness are.

By enumerating the number of times, "twice, three times," that God rescues people (33:29), Elihu is not limiting the number of times God extends mercy, but is stressing God's *repeated* efforts to save, something that is mostly absent from the remarks of all the other characters in the book, including Yahweh. Eliphaz had said "happy is the one whom God reproves . . . for he wounds, but he binds up . . . he will deliver even those who are guilty" (5:17–18; 22:30), but it is not a point that he emphasized. Only Elihu's teachings evoke a response of joy. He says there is freshness, joy, and singing (33:25–27) by the recipient of mercy, who can say "my life shall see the light" (33:28).

Elihu's mercy-dominated approach really does offer a solution to the impasse between Job and his friends. Elihu pictures the repentant believer whose righteousness is vindicated ("he restores

117. Hartley, *Book of Job*, 447.

a person's righteousness," 33:26b NABRE), and whose sin is for-
given (who "perverted what was right, and it was not paid back to
me," 33:27b). The vindication affirms an aspect of Job's argument,
while the sin-admission confirms an aspect of the friends' position, but without the extreme claims of either opinion (that Job
is either completely innocent or deeply sinful). Elihu's position is
more mature theologically than that of any of the Dialogue part-
ners. He argues that God's whole attitude is one of mercy: "to bring
back their souls from the Pit, so that they may see the light of life"
(33:30). This is a truth that was simply overlooked by both Job and
his friends, who were obsessed with the question of justice.

Some of Elihu's words imply at least partial acceptance of the
doctrine that sickness and affliction are the consequences of sin,
a common belief in the ancient world, and an especially intense
belief in wisdom literature, as seen in the words of Eliphaz, sometimes of Job himself, in Proverbs[118] (or at least a certain simplistic
interpretation of Proverbs), and in the wisdom literature of Egypt.
Job had attacked this teaching. We must await later teachers to
hear that evil falls upon the just and the unjust, and that the justice
of God is not shattered by this painful fact of life. Elihu is too much
a man of his time to rise wholly above the teaching that health is a
reward and sickness a punishment. What is unusual is his emphasis that God rescues these people even though they were *not* innocent (vv. 17, 27), and that he will do it "twice, three times" (v. 29).

The Elihu character is hoping to get Job to look at his suffering in a new way, to see that it is probably God's way of trying to
reach him or save him. Elihu offers no explanation of Job's *particular* plight, but presents the attitude God has toward *any* sufferer: wanting to save, ready to provide a ransom, ready to restore
righteousness and joy. "Elihu is telling Job that God has not been
silent, but has been speaking to him in many ways through his
dreams and his pains."[119]

Elihu's emphasis on God's mercy is remarkable, and the
brightness of his language is striking; the recipient says "my life

118. Prov 3:6, 26; 16:5; 22:4, 8.
119. Hartley, *Book of Job*, 449.

shall see the light . . . the light of life" (vv. 28, 30). By saying "I desire to justify you," Elihu is wanting to make Job just (the literal
meaning of the Piel verb with the second person masculine suffix
צִדְּקֶךָ *tsadᵉqekhā* in v. 32[120]), which evidently goes along with being
rescued and restored, or accepted and redeemed, in vv. 26 and 28.
This is hardly treating Job as an enemy.

Elihu is confronting what ails Job. He is not out to put Job
down, but to show him what is delaying his healing; he has already
stated that none of Job's interlocutors confute him (32:12)—nor
do they help him, but Elihu will! Positioning his intrusion in the
text where he does, Elihu implies that the truths he utters are what
make the happy ending possible. He may not be able to satisfy Job's
argument with providence theology (the notion that God always
rewards the just and punishes the unjust in this lifetime), but he
can offer answers that focus on God's generosity.

There is no need to go to trial with God since God is willing to
rescue even the guilty. Elihu has no theodicy to offer, only salvation:
Job should give up on theodicy and accept the revealed mercy.

The justice of God (chapter 34)

Elihu teaches that people *can* listen and learn wisdom (33:33), *can*
"choose what is right" (34:4), in fact, "you must choose" (34:33).
People *can* be taught by God. They can pray "teach me what I do
not see" (34:32). He is optimistic about the human ability to call
upon God's power to rescue and restore. We must not overlook
this when assessing his critique of Job.

Elihu's criticisms of Job start to get harsher in this chapter.
Job "drinks up scoffing like water" (34:7), perhaps scoffing at good
advice. Further, Job "walks with the wicked" (34:8).[121] It seems that
"Elihu is now caught in the same logic as the friends. By affirming

---

120. Piel infinitive construct of *tsadaq* with second-person masculine sin-
gular object suffix; Owens, *Analytical Key*, 3:231; Dhorme, *Commentary*, 507.

121. "What Eliphaz has implied about Job, Elihu says bluntly" (Hartley,
Book of Job, 452).

that God's ways cannot be questioned, he is forced to denounce Job's opinions as impious."[122]

To Job's apparent opinion that being right with God brings no profit, since God does not give a man his due (34:9; perhaps paraphrasing Job from 9:22; 21:7), Elihu insists that God is never unjust (34:11–12) or partial (v. 19). Actually, Job had never said exactly those things, but Elihu reframes Job's remarks in a more negative version. Elihu insists that God misses nothing of what mortals do (vv. 21–25); and "he heard the cry of the afflicted" (v. 28). All one has to do is *ask to be taught*: "Teach me what I do not see; if I have done iniquity, I will do it no more" (34:32). This involves humility and openness. One simply admits one's inadequacy and asks for help. Wisdom comes as a direct revelation from God ("teach me," הֹרֵנִי, *horēni*, the Hiphil imperative form of יָרָה). It makes sense to admit that there is much that one does not see, and to ask for God's help to see it. God supports our life constantly. In fact, if God withdrew his spirit, everyone would die (34:14–15).

The teaching on suffering is linked to a notion of repentance; suffering is interpreted as "punishment" for an offense in v. 31, but the solution is to sin no more, to admit that one has done iniquity, and ask to be taught (v. 32). Again we see that one must readily admit on principle and without argument to one's inadequacy, even to spiritual blindness. Elihu sees this as a sensible response to the absolute sovereignty and generosity of God.

One might paraphrase this line of reasoning by saying that Job would do better to assume the role of a student who needs guidance, than of a defendant who thinks he can bring charges against God and win the case. His continual arguing with God is dangerous and impious; it smacks of rebellion (vv. 35–37). Here is where Elihu's criticisms of Job become unfair, by misconceiving Job's motives. It is unfair to say of Job that "his answers are those of the wicked. For he adds rebellion to his sin" (vv. 36–37). Elihu is not immune to the ancient practice of making summary judgments. He simply cannot understand Job's struggle, and takes no notice of Job's faith-breakthroughs in chapters 14 and 19 in the

122. Andersen, *Job*, 271.

direction of affirming an afterlife that is something other than the gloomy condition of shades, the Mesopotamian-influenced view that Job and his friends seem to take for granted.

To appreciate Job one must appreciate the occasional break-throughs in his struggle against the overwhelming pressure of prevailing views. But Elihu seems blissfully unaware of such struggle. He "fails to allow for the particulars of an individual case."[123]

The perfection of God (chapters 35–36)

Vicchio points out that Elihu makes eleven references to the Divine in these chapters, "including his employment of *El, Elohim, Eloah, Shaddai, Kabbir*, and two references to 'Maker,' at 35:10 . . . the Hebrew *a'sah* [and] at 36:3, the Hebrew *pa'al*, a noun form of the verb 'to make.'"[124]

Elihu's vocabulary may be diverse and colorful, but his remarks are starting to become more predictable and his stance more argumentative; he pursues Job's litigiousness, his attempt to be "right before God" (35:2). He issues stern warnings against despair—not something that is usually very helpful to the despairing. He says Job overlooks the fact that his actions do not affect God very much (35:6–7).

Elihu is not interested in the question of whether Job sinned in the past, but only that Job has said inappropriate things in his speeches. He addresses Job's tendency to complain and to challenge God, but he seems unfair when he says "God does not hear an empty cry . . . how much less when you say that you do not see him" (35:13–14). Job had indeed cried out "I cannot behold him . . . I cannot see him . . . I cry to you and you do not answer" (23:9; 30:20), but these are honest outbursts of the seeker, and not dogmatic assertions that God *cannot* be found.[125]

123. Hartley, *Book of Job*, 462.

124. Vicchio, *Job*, 241–42.

125. See Boss, *Human Consciousness*, 173.

Elihu says Job is failing to notice God's non-vengefulness, his tendency to "not punish, and he does not greatly heed transgression" (35:15). Thus, Job's negativism looks foolish. Elihu confronts Job's tendency to spiral downward into complaint, to generate "empty talk" (v. 16).

Mercy does return to the discussion: God "does not despise any"; he "gives the afflicted their right [*mishpat*]" (36:5–6), his eyes are on the righteous (36:7), and he shows people whenever "they are behaving arrogantly. He opens their ears to instruction, and commands that they return from iniquity" (36:9–10). These are "good people who go to the bad and need rescuing."[126] God takes the initiative to instruct people and put them back on the right path. Andersen finally sees something he likes in Elihu. He says chapter 36 "contains Elihu's best and most distinctive ideas," showing "a deeper analysis and a more humane sensitivity" than his other speeches.[127] This chapter shows what Vicchio calls "the moral qualities view, whereby suffering acts as a kind of discipline for developing certain moral traits like trust and fortitude."[128]

These compassionate ideas transcend anything uttered by Job or the friends—or by Yahweh in the final chapters. Elihu's teaching is the high point in the doctrine of God in the book of Job. "He delivers the afflicted by their affliction, and opens their ear by adversity [בַּלַּחַץ *balachats*]" (36:15). Suffering, therefore, can be an avenue for God's instruction. Suffering is not deserved, but it is an opportunity for God to reach us ("the moral qualities view"[129]). A rabbinic comment illuminates this. The Gaon Saadiah insists that what Elihu teaches is that Job's suffering is *not* deserved, and yet God makes use of it. If it were really God's wrath, there would be no escape from it.[130]

---

126. Clines, *Job 21–37*, 856. Clines finds this more realistic than the simplistic division into good and bad people found in other wisdom literature.

127. Andersen, *Job*, 278.

128. Vicchio, *Job*, 248.

129. Vicchio, *Job*, 398.

130. Saadiah, *Book of Theodicy*, 370.

Kaufman sees Elihu's monologue as an affirmation of God's love, and he sees an anthropological proof of God's love: "Can a God who implanted in man moral consciousness be Himself indifferent to moral demands? Job's very sense of moral outrage is an outcome of God's goodness (chapter 35)."[131] Kaufman may be correct, but it is also true that Elihu's scolding tone tends to undermine the possibility of Job understanding his experience as a manifestation of love. Elihu's arrogance also comes through here: "For truly my words are not false; one who is perfect [תְּמִים *temim*] in knowledge is with you" (36:4).

But Elihu clearly wants to help Job see the generosity of God, "for I have yet something to say on God's behalf" (36:2). God is kindly (v. 5); he does not withhold a man's rights, "but gives the afflicted their right" (v. 6), while he shows people whenever "they are behaving arrogantly" (v. 9). At that point, "He opens their ears to instruction" (v. 10). Obviously, then, God is "a teacher" (36:22).

Elihu wants to emphasize God's eagerness to save. If God can persuade sinners to repent, to obey and serve God, then "they complete their days in prosperity" (36:11). To some degree, this echoes the prosperity theology of that day. But what is interesting is that God is bringing affliction *in order to instruct and to save.* Not retribution, but salvation, is his purpose. "He delivers the afflicted by their affliction" (v. 15). Even Edwin Good (usually very negative about Elihu) must admit that this goes beyond anything found elsewhere in the book: "Suffering . . . has become the rescuing experience itself, the means by which . . . restoration takes place."[132]

Elihu finishes off this chapter by emphasizing that God is great and unfathomable beyond our knowing (vv. 22–26), he commands the sea and sky (vv. 29–33), and he provides food to people (v. 31), all of which anticipates Yahweh's self-description in the book's final chapters.

---

131. Kaufmann, "Job the Righteous Man," 69.

132. Good, *In Turns of Tempest,* 333.

Elihu pre-responds to God (chapter 37)

In chapter 37 we find Elihu using naturalistic illustrations: God "thunders" (v. 5); he sends ice, the whirlwind, and rain (vv. 9–11); and he afflicts either "for correction, or for his land, or for love" (37:13). Pope points out that the noun, "land," is unexpected, that a theological term would be expected between "correction" and "love"; he suggests "grace." He sees the *aleph* at the beginning of *'arṣô* as a prefix, rather than part of the noun. What is left is רצו, *rṣw*, a Palmyrene deity, whose nickname is "grace."[133] That may be a stretch, but the dictionaries have a noun, רָצוֹן *rāṣon*, which means "favor,"[134] and a verb רָצָה, *rāṣā*, which means "be well-disposed toward"[135] or "be pleased with."[136] In any case, 37:13 speaks of God issuing his commands for correction, for love, and either "for his land" or "for grace." Once again, Elihu emphasizes God's active mercy, his intervening to try to save people.

In a passage that anticipates the theophany, Elihu advises Job to "stop and consider the wondrous works of God," to realize that he doesn't "know the balancing of the clouds" or how God sends the lightning (37:14–16). We don't know how God works his commands (vv. 15–16, 18); due to our ignorance, we do not know how to bring a case before God (v. 19); as one cannot look at the sun, so one cannot look on God's "awesome majesty" (vv. 21–22); we cannot figure him out; it is important to stress that the Almighty "is great in power *and* justice," and is never unjust, for "abundant righteousness he will not violate" (37:23). Hartley observes, "Power and justice, so often divided on earth, are inexorably bound together in God."[137] Elihu emphasizes human powerlessness, but without losing sight of the goodness of God. There is no injustice in God.

133. Pope, *Job*, 278, 283–84.

134. Holladay, *Concise Hebrew*, 345–46; BDB 953.

135. Holladay, *Concise Hebrew*, 345.

136. BDB 953.

137. Hartley, *Book of Job*, 484.

There are several reasons to accept that Elihu is first of all a *reader* of the book of Job, and that he wrote and added his material to an existing text of the Job. One indication is that chapters 36–37 anticipate and echo the grandeur and naturalism of the theophany of the final chapters. Also, when he starts speaking to Job, he tells Job that he has no reason to fear him, "no fear of *me* need terrify you" (33:7), which seems to be distinguishing his approach from the domineering demeanor of Yahweh in the final chapters. He asks Job if he understands the wonders of God (37:15, 18), just as Yahweh will later do (38:4), but the purpose seems to be to get Job to realize that God does not torment the good man, and so the wise fear him (37:23–24). Of course, this returns us to the original problem, that Job *is* a good man, and yet is being tormented.

Elihu's Rhetoric

Elihu's vocabulary is theologically rich. He uses more names for the Deity than any other character in the book, "from *El, Eloah,* and *Elohim,* as well as *Shaddai,*" and he uses the word "Power" (*khoach*) to refer to God in 37:23.[138] He uses far more words related to righteousness, understanding, and justice than do any of the other characters.[139]

Elihu's teachings about God are consistently positive. He is impatient with what seem to him to be immature or extreme positions, one conformist and conservative, the other nonconformist and radical. He seeks to transcend the question of justice to attain a more mature philosophy that takes notice of God's profound graciousness and empathy.

We sophisticated moderns who love to obsess upon ambiguity, irony, and frustration, need to ask whether our theodicy is not infected with negativism. When our theodicy asks "why does God allow evil?" is our emphasis upon *God* or upon *evil*? If on the

---

138. Vicchio, *Job*, 214.
139. Vicchio, *Job*, 215.

latter, we tend to get lost in the mental coils of complaint, and we dampen our own spiritual receptivity.

Elihu does not answer the theodicy question to the satisfaction of anyone who is *obsessed with evil* (as he admits in 36:17). His focus is on the generosity of God, which Job and Job's friends are overlooking. The answer to the problem of evil is not to be found in obsessing about the problem, but in recognizing the real nature of God, despite the suffering. Elihu, young man that he is, is not able to say this in a terribly sophisticated manner, but he can give the honest affirmation that God "is gracious" (33:24).

Vicchio notes that Elihu offers much theology that is simply not present in the three friends' speeches. Elihu says "that God uses evil and suffering in order to develop certain, significant moral qualities, such as patience and fortitude," and Vicchio cites 36:15, where "he delivers the afflicted by their affliction."[140] Vicchio sees Elihu effectively reversing the approach of the three friends. "Elihu shifts the theological debate from looking backward (retributive justice) to looking forward (divine plan)."[141]

We should emphasize that, for Elihu, instruction comes *directly* from God. God intervenes and teaches people: "He opens their ears to instruction" (36:10). The person who prays "comes into [God's] presence with joy" (33:26). God shows us our transgressions, and seeks to open our ears (36:9–10, 15). This is a revelatory soteriology. Elihu puts an emphasis on lived experience, where one lives with an openness to God's gracious outreach. Despite the pompous tone of some of Elihu's remarks, his theology offers an interesting emphasis on God's kindly interaction with mortals, sometimes mediated by an angel.

Vicchio suggests that the Elihu monologue includes "the 'moral qualities view,' the 'test perspective,' and the 'divine plan theory.'"[142] The test perspective pictures Job as coming through the test successfully. The divine plan view sees God as knowing the

---

140. Vicchio, *Job*, 212.

141. Vicchio, *Job*, 214.

142. Vicchio, *Job*, 212.

meaning of suffering and how it will turn out (33:12; 34:31–32; 36:22, 26–30; 37:23–24).[143] God knows the end from the beginning.

The main problem with Elihu is his overconfidence and his impatience with Job's expressions of distress. He ridicules other positions than his own, and offers his own as the only rational understanding. He can end up seeming "dogmatic" and "rigid."[144] Nevertheless, his contribution to the book is unique, and, if the reader can provide the sensitivity that Elihu lacks, and an ability to balance different viewpoints, then Elihu's theology can be very helpful.

Dating the Elihu section is particularly difficult. Vicchio says "the vocabulary of Elihu looks far more like postexilic Judaism than does the rest of the book"; it contains the highest concentration of *hapax legomena* in the book of Job, and "many more Aramaisms" than in the rest of the book.[145] I think Elihu is a very ancient writer, possibly prior to the Hebrew monarchy, but his words, as we have them, have been reworked by a postexilic editor, who is responsible for the postexilic vocabulary and the Aramaisms. There is a simplicity and primitivism to Elihu's rhetoric that speaks of an early period. There is no appearance of prophetic ideas such as *ḥesed* (lovingkindness), covenant renewal, the law written on the heart, Zion being saved and corrected, just rule from a new Davidic ruler, exile, or return from exile. Elihu's ideas are from an earlier period, I think.

Medieval Jewish Philosophers

A number of medieval Jewish philosophers saw Elihu as the supremely wise sage in the book of Job. The first one, chronologically, is Saadiah Gaon, who taught that there are three kinds of suffering, one for discipline and instruction, such as a father might impose; the next is as punishment for sin, which is also instructional; third is a trial that God can inflict on the innocent to enable the latter to

143. Vicchio, *Job*, 213.

144. Newsom, "Job," 579.

145. Vicchio, *Job*, 214; some *hapax legomena* found in 32:6; 33:9, 24–25; 34:36; 35:15; 36:27; 37:9. On the Aramaisms, see Vicchio, 214, 388.

earn reward by his acceptance of affliction. Saadiah sees Elihu as teaching that God can bring trials upon the righteous, and reward them if they pass the test.[146] Saadiah's Elihu argues "that three types of individuals receive reward in the afterlife: one who repents of his sins after God causes him to suffer, one who repents before he suffers, and one who has no sins whatsoever but is made to suffer as a test of his faith."[147] Job fits in the third category, but he is not allowed to know in which category he falls, or the test won't work. His trial is still ongoing as Elihu speaks and even as God speaks, later.

The twelfth-century Jewish philosopher Maimonides had quite a bit to say about Job and about the problem of evil. One thing he does is delineate several different sources of evil. First there are natural disasters like earthquakes and volcanoes, over which humans have no control. Second are the evils of human violence, over which other humans sometimes have limited control, and sometimes have no control.[148] Violent people act out of free will, and can hurt innocent people.

Third are those evils that are self-inflicted, the result of immoderation, alcohol abuse, and other misbehaviors, for which God is not to blame. An Aristotelian, Maimonides puts an emphasis on rationality. He "uses Job as a model for the transformation" that nonphilosophical Jews need to experience.[149] He concludes that Job *did* come to a right understanding of suffering; he "attains intellectual virtue as a result of his trials . . . Intellectual perfection—the ability to concentrate on God while conducting one's worldly affairs—allows a person to develop a resistance to suffering . . . the ability to become impervious to physical affliction."[150] "Job learns . . . an inner psychological resistance or immunity to suffering."[151] Suffering helps to wean Job from his false belief in wealth, family, and health as the sources of happiness. He learns in

146. Eisen, *Book of Job in Medieval*, 21.

147. Eisen, *Book of Job in Medieval*, 27.

148. Adams, *Redefining Job*, 105; citing *Guide for the Perplexed* 3:12.

149. Eisen, *Book of Job in Medieval*, 211.

150. Adams, *Redefining Job*, 106–7.

151. Eisen, *Book of Job in Medieval*, 65.

the end that happiness only comes from intellectual virtue.[152] This is what I call an unsatisfactory answer. Despite the desirability of wisdom and intellectual virtue, they do not remove the pain of the loss of family and health. In the end, this answer seems excessively abstract and elitist.

Maimonides's contemporary Ibn Tibbon follows in his footsteps, philosophically, although his exegesis of Job differs at certain points: for instance, he disagrees with Maimonides's view that Job has achieved intellectual perfection by the end of the book.[153] Ibn Tibbon agrees with Maimonides in seeing the goal of human living in intellectual perfection, but he says that this issues in immortality, and therefore "that true providence is immortality"; further, "the afterlife is equated with the immortality of the intellect."[154] His thinking is lofty and abstract. "True providence is immortality."[155] The sparing of the soul mentioned in 33:18, he felt, was a reference to "immortality of intellect."[156] For Ibn Tibbon, God is not punishing Job,[157] nor is he testing Job. Suffering comes from the natural order, and it tends to teach a person to value the intellectual virtues, "by convincing the individual that attachment to physical and material things is futile and that he should pursue intellectual perfection so as to achieve immortality."[158]

Eisen shows that Ibn Tibbon had an influence on later Jewish philosophers, although they do not mention Tibbon by name. However, they do repeat his concept "that immortality of the intellect is the only form of providence."[159] It seems that the afterlife will consist of detached thinking by perfected intellects, possibly as dry

152. Adams, *Redefining Job*, 107.

153. Eisen, *Book of Job in Medieval*, 103.

154. Eisen, *Book of Job in Medieval*, 97.

155. Eisen, *Book of Job in Medieval*, 87.

156. Eisen, *Book of Job in Medieval*, 86.

157. Ibn Tibbon "is firmly at odds with the retributive justice of the Torah" (Eisen, *Book of Job in Medieval*, 227).

158. Eisen, *Book of Job in Medieval*, 87.

159. Eisen, *Book of Job in Medieval*, 108; Eisen is referring to the writings of Isaac Arundi here.

as the dust of the old Sheol concept. Maimonides and his followers seem to understand the "angel" mentioned by Elihu (33:23) as either natural forces or as the Active Intellect:[160] that which enables pure and truthful reflection, in the Aristotelian worldview.

Another important Jewish thinker has his base of operations in Rome. Zeraḥiah Ḥen understands Elihu in chapter 33 to be giving the true interpretation of providence, but it is beyond Job's comprehension, so Elihu reverts to an angle, in chapters 34–37, where he encourages Job to unquestioningly accept his lot and not rail against God.[161] According to Zeraḥiah, Job has decent moral character, but lacks the intellectual capacity to really understand Elihu's teachings on providence.

For these and other medieval Jewish philosophers, Elihu is the supreme philosopher, although they are largely projecting their own views upon Elihu. They admire what they perceive to be Elihu's intellectual virtue. They share Elihu's view that one should always affirm God's justice.

What Elihu Offers Us

Job's questions are the most compellingly dramatic part of the play. They articulate the feelings, worries, and reactions that many people have experienced in times of pain. Without a doubt, Job is the character with whom most readers of Job identify. But I insist that the book would not be complete without Elihu, and in a certain sense, Elihu has the last word. While Yahweh has the last word in the narrative sequence, it is Elihu who inserted his views last, implying dissatisfaction with the "shut up and submit" message of the Yahweh speeches.

Elihu's message culminates with a linkage of God's power and love: If we can realize that *everything* God does is either "for

160. Eisen, *Book of Job in Medieval*, 59, 89–90, 123.
161. Eisen, *Book of Job in Medieval*, 125–27, 133–34.

discipline, or for grace, or for mercy" (Job 37:13, Pope's translation[162]), then we have reached a place of mature trusting.

While we may identify with Job, we must listen to Elihu, who vehemently affirms the goodness of God. While Job draws us in with his thoughts about injustice (and an appeal to our pity), Elihu appeals to our soul and to our thoughtful spirituality (devoid of self-pity). Elihu is our instructor; he gives the best answers to Job's questions that can be obtained without a discussion of the afterlife. If we add Job's own intimations of the afterlife in chapters 14 and 19 to Elihu's teaching of the compassion of God, we get considerably more comprehensive answers than those that the Yahweh of chapters 38 to 41 gives, although those responses, too, must be factored in, since there will always be a huge area of human ignorance, and it is best to accept the wisdom and power of God as a given.

With his many remarks about God's efforts to reach people, Elihu is offering a revelatory soteriology, a message of hope and faith.

THE LORD'S RESPONSE

In chapter 38, the Lord appears "out of the whirlwind" (38:1). It is to be noted that the name of the deity becomes Yahweh, and not El, Eloah, or Shaddai, as throughout the Dialogue. Yahweh begins by rebuking Job: "Who is this that darkens counsel by words without knowledge?"

My biggest disappointment in reading Job for the first time was Yahweh's answer from the whirlwind. Yahweh's rejoinder answers none of Job's questions nor his desire for a summary judgment. Yahweh's reply seems designed to intimidate, to hammer Job with an awareness of his ignorance and powerlessness. "Where were you when I laid the foundation of the earth?" (38:3). Well, obviously, nowhere. "Who determined its measurements—surely you know!" (38:4). The response seems unnecessarily sarcastic. As in the Prologue, there is a reference to heavenly beings: "when the

162. Pope, *Job*, 278.

morning stars sang together and all the heavenly beings shouted for joy" (38:7). "Have you commanded the morning since your days began . . . ?" (38:12). "Do you know the ordinances of the heavens?" (38:33). Well, of course not.

Verses 31–32 mention some constellations, but the underlying message is the same as above: "Can you bind the chains of the Pleiades, or loose the cords of Orion? Can you lead forth the Mazzaroth in their season, or can you guide the Bear with its children?" Mazzaroth may be a particular astronomic entity, such as Venus or the Hyades,[163] or the Corona Borealis;[164] it is a hapax legomenon: a word that occurs only once in the Bible.[165]

The Lord seems to be bludgeoning Job with pronouncements of his finitude. Is this meant to induce *fear* of God, without any basis for *loving* God? Newsom sees implications of divine care in this speech. The statements show not only God controlling the boundary between order and disorder, but also showing a *caring* hand in restraining the dangerous sea (38:11).[166]

In 38:36, Yahweh says "Who has put wisdom in the inward parts, or given understanding to the mind?" However, the terms that NRSV renders "inward parts" and "mind" are quite uncertain. "Inward parts" (טֻחוֹת, *tuchot*) might be a fairly secure translation,[167] and is its meaning in Psalm 51:6 NRSV (51:8 MT), but some scholars raise the possibility that it refers to the Egyptian god of wisdom, Thoth.[168] The other term, שֶׂכְוִי, *sekᵉwî* is less certain; Dhorme thinks it refers to the cock, finding an ibis and a cock in that verse.[169] Newsom accepts the "ibis" and "cock" interpretation, signifying the rising of the Nile and the coming of the rain, respectively,[170] al-

---

163. Pope, *Job*, 301. As Hyades: Boss, *Human Consciousness*, 190.

164. Dhorme, *Commentary*, 590.

165. Vicchio, *Job*, 262.

166. Newsom, *Book of Job*, 242, 244.

167. BDB 376.

168. Pope, *Job*, 302; Boss, *Human Consciousness*, 191.

169. Dhorme, *Commentary*, 591–93

170. Newsom, "Job," 605.

though Gordis finds it unlikely.[171] Andersen is also skeptical "that pagan gods would turn up in a book so ruthlessly monotheistic."[172] The sentence can make perfectly good sense either with NRSV's "inward parts" and "mind," or with Dhorme's "ibis" and "cock." There is plenty of naturalistic imagery in the surrounding verses, but there is no reason Yahweh could not mention the reasoning power of human beings.

Janzen draws out a positive message from the final chapters. He says that the whirlwind is "the autumn sirocco that signals the coming of the rejuvenating rains," and sees Yahweh as drawing Job "back into the web of a rejuvenated creation."[173] The story shows that God is generous in blessing.

Vicchio draws out a philosophic implication of the Yahweh speeches by focusing on "counsel" in 38:2. The "Hebrew term *'esa* . . . also means 'Plan,'" and, in fact, "the divine plan view is the overall response to evil and suffering to be found in the God speeches."[174] However, I find Yahweh in these chapters to be doing more taunting than teaching. The only parts of any plan that are explicated are those that concern animals and natural phenomena. Job has sought justice. Instead, what he gets are messages about his smallness and God's immensity.

The reader cannot help but notice that the Yahweh speech is imperious, contemptuous, and impatient. But we could also say that Yahweh is answering Job's prayer that the Lord should respond, and that the Lord is speaking "out of concern for his servant," to correct him, not to condemn him.[175] He ignores Job's questions about his suffering, not to mention his more disturbing questions about God's justice, but the Lord does not ignore the request to get *some* kind of response from the Deity. He calls Job foolish and insignificant, but does not accuse Job of any sins, yet. There will be a confrontational question in the next speech of Yahweh.

171. Gordis, *Book of God*, 453.

172. Andersen, *Job*, 301.

173. Janzen, "Blessing and Justice," 68.

174. Vicchio, *Job*, 257–58.

175. Hartley, *Book of Job*, 487.

Here, the taunting continues, as Yahweh asks if Job knows the secrets of, or provides the sustenance for, various animals and birds in 38:39—39:30. "Is it at your command that the eagle mounts up and makes its nest on high? . . . Shall a fault-finder contend with the Almighty?" (39:27; 40:2). This last remark seems to really get through to Job, and he admits "See, I am of small account; what shall I answer you?" (40:4). Daniel Timmer prefers "I am flawed and finite" for the first part of 40:4.[176] This may be the turning point in the whole drama, where Job realizes that he *has* sinned in his prideful insistence on his own innocence, implying that he knows better than God. Edwin Good writes, "He has accused God of immorality and injustice in punishing the innocent as well as the guilty. But the base of the argument all along has been Job's own righteousness, the fact that he deserves justification. In the interests of his own fate, Job would be prepared to dethrone God."[177] He has been arguing on the basis of "the magical power of morality,"[178] seeking to compel God to respond. He had "demanded acquittal of an unknown and nonexistent sin. He received acquittal of a known and admitted one."[179] Good finds this to be healthy irony at the end of the book of Job. Job needs God's forgiveness after all, and needs to stop asserting his own absolute innocence. Good's analysis is thought-provoking and coherent, although I am not fully convinced.

Not going as far as Edwin Good does, I will say that I see Job accepting his smallness and God's greatness, recognizing that God does care enough to address him personally, and coming to accept God and wherever his relationship with God may stand. As of this point in the story, there is no hint that Job's wealth will be restored. He has a spiritual experience before that ever happens. He has had his good relationship with God restored, and that is what matters the most to him. This is an emotionally

---

176. Timmer, "God's Speeches," 294.

177. Good, *Irony*, 238.

178. Good, *Irony*, 243.

179. Good, *Irony*, 240.

powerful moment in the story. There is still considerable uncertainty as to how the story will end.

Job's response gives God the opening to deliver a second speech, again "out of the whirlwind" (40:6). At first it addresses an important issue in Job's behavior: "Will you even put me in the wrong? Will you condemn me that you may be justified?" (40:8). This is the closest Yahweh gets to possibly accusing Job of sin. What follows is another naturalistic observation like those we had in chapters 38–39: "Have you an arm like God, and can you thunder with a voice like his?" (40:9). But the next stanza does deal with moral issues. Yahweh raises a hypothetical situation where Job is called upon to bring low the proud, to tread down the wicked, to bind them "in the world below" (40:12–13). Yahweh's point is that Job does not really have this power; if he did, then "your own right hand can give you victory," presumably meaning victory in the debate (40:14). This is telling Job, and all people, that they are being presumptuous whenever they think they know better than God.

Another interpretation is that Yahweh is inviting Job into partnership with him in opposing evil, to "tread down the wicked" (40:12).[180] After discussing 42:8, I will return to André LaCocque's proposition.

Yahweh moves on to a long speech about Job's powerlessness to control the frightening beasts Behemoth and Leviathan, apparently to impress Job with the power of these creatures. Of Behemoth: "Its bones are tubes of bronze, its limbs like bars of iron" (40:18). It seems likely that the term originally referred to an actual animal like a hippopotamus, and Leviathan to a crocodile,[181] but ongoing speculation about Behemoth and Leviathan had reached mythological or supernatural levels.

Job's powerlessness is emphasized in the speech about Leviathan: "Can you draw out Leviathan with a fish-hook, or press down its tongue with a cord? . . . Will it make many supplications to you? Will it speak soft words to you?" (41:1, 3). In Ugaritic mythology, Baal kills "Lotan, the Fleeting Serpent," and in another text, it is

180. LaCocque, "Deconstruction," 90.
181. Vicchio, *Job*, 277–78; Pope, *Job*, 320.

Anat who destroys the Serpent.[182] Pope and some other scholars are convinced that Leviathan is a mythological creature.[183] Andersen thinks they are creatures in nature, though the author has taken poetic license in describing their powers.[184] "Its underparts are like sharp potsherds . . . On earth it has no equal" (41:30, 33). So what? What does that have to do with why the wicked prosper? Nothing. It is just another illustration that God is more powerful than any creature.

The possible mythological character of Leviathan may explain the strangely polytheistic mention "When it raises itself up the gods (*eliym*) are afraid" (41:25), which, for Pope, recalls the time in the Gilgamesh Epic where the gods became frightened by the deluge, or the Mesopotamian Creation Epic, where the gods express fear and distress.[185] Some translators prefer "the mighty" (NIV, NASB, Aquila, Symmachus, the Targum[186]), instead of "the gods." Either way, it does nothing to answer Job's questions.

The speeches say something about God's relationship to chaos and creation. They are building up an atmosphere of "sublime terror."[187] It does *not* show God establishing order by destroying the chaos monsters.[188] It is not a triumphalist narrative. In fact, "the uncomfortable sense grows that God's identification with the chaotic is as strong as with the symbols of order."[189] John Schneider feels that these speeches show that "God is working *in and through* disorder to bring about his ordered cosmos."[190] God is in control, but evil still exists and is part of the whole picture.[191]

182. Vicchio, *Job*, 279; Pope, *Job*, 329.

183. Pope, *Job*, 329–32; Vicchio, *Job*, 279.

184. Andersen, *Job*, 310–12.

185. Pope, *Job*, 344.

186. Pope, *Job*, 344.

187. Newsom, *Book of Job*, 243.

188. Newsom, *Book of Job*, 248–49.

189. Newsom, *Book of Job*, 252.

190. Schneider, "Seeing God Where," 255.

191. Schneider, "Seeing God Where," 255–56.

To derive spiritual value from these chapters, we have to take a different approach than the approach of theodicy that seeks intellectually fulsome answers. What seems to matter here is that God finally *speaks to Job*, and convinces Job to trust God and no longer to try to put him "in the wrong" (40:8). Some interpreters are not bothered by the fact that God never answers Job's questions. What is key, they say, is that God appears to Job, and so "the rebellious hero here becomes a joyous confessor . . . He no longer needs a rational theodicy. He is ready to believe without understanding."[192] "Job's questions have not been answered, but he is now satisfied that God—who seemed to him to be a stranger—is still on his side."[193] Job no longer needs to focus on his own problems, because "he now *discovers a God-centric universe*. And here he finds faith and self-forgetfulness."[194]

After God's second speech, Job acknowledges God's power (42:2) and admits that he had reached for things beyond his understanding (42:3). The appearance of God has made a difference: "I had heard of you by the hearing of the ear, but now my eye sees you; therefore I despise myself, and repent in dust and ashes" (42:5–6). Job is not admitting to having committed real wickedness, but to having overreached and to having uttered foolish words.[195] Oesterley and Robinson say that "This is no solution of the problem, and the poet cannot have intended it to be understood as one"; there *is* no solution. "The sufferer has seen God, and that is enough."[196] "The complete evasion of the issue as Job has posed it must be the poet's oblique way of admitting that there is no satisfactory answer available to man, apart from faith."[197] Similarly, Rowley says Job's "intellectual problem is left unsolved, but he has transcended it."[198]

192. Oesterley and Robinson, "Three Stages," 212–13.

193. Kynes and Kynes, *Wrestling with Job*, 189.

194. Belitsos, *Truths about Evil*, 255.

195. Andersen, *Job*, 314–15.

196. Oesterley and Robinson, "Three Stages," 216.

197. Pope, *Job*, lxxx.

198. Rowley, "Intellectual Versus Spiritual," 342.

The "I despise myself" of 42:6 NRSV seems to be wrong. The verb אֶמְאַס, 'emas does not have an object here; the word "myself" does not appear. The meaning could be "I retract"[199] or "I reject"[200] or "I recant,"[201] rather than "I despise myself." Retraction, rather than self-loathing, is the idea for this verb. Holladay gives "disavowal (thus rejection) of earlier words."[202] Job has been convinced to stop complaining. He senses that he was overly confrontational and brazen, and that he needs to "take it back." It is not that he is admitting to being an infamous sinner, but rather "that Job repents primarily of his frailty as it came to expression at various points in his speeches of chapters 3—31, obscuring, doubting, and impugning God's justice."[203] It is also his overconfidence and self-centeredness that he now rejects. He has been maintaining his own innocence (29:12–25), recounting his history as being "like a king among his troops" (29:25); he has placed himself "on his own pedestal."[204] What he learns from the divine speeches is that God provides for all living things out of generosity, not as a reward for righteousness. "Blessings are signs of divine grace, not reward."[205]

At 42:7 the book reverts to prose, like the book's Prologue. The Lord rebukes Eliphaz and "your two friends; for you have not spoken of me what is right, as my servant Job has" (42:7). What was "right" in what Job said? All the many arguments and complaints? Probably not. Timmer says that it is, specifically, Job's repentance in 42:6 that is being referenced.[206] He has gained "a more robust view of God's justice and integrity."[207] The point, according to Timmer, is that reverence is the prerequisite of wisdom. Job

199. Vicchio, *Job*, 293. Boss has "turn away from" (*Human Consciousness*, 244n6).

200. Timmer, "God's Speeches," 299; Joo, "Biblical Atlas," 82.

201. Pope, *Job*, 347–48.

202. Holladay, *Concise Hebrew*, 180.

203. Timmer, "God's Speeches," 300.

204. Joo, "Biblical Atlas," 77.

205. Joo, "Biblical Atlas," 83.

206. Timmer, "God's Speeches," 302–3.

207. Timmer, "God's Speeches," 304.

finally demonstrates that reverence in 42:6, and is acknowledged by Yahweh in 42:7–8.

The principal characters in this interaction are Yahweh, Job, and the three friends. Neither Elihu nor the satan are mentioned. In the story of Job, Elihu is important intellectually and theologically, but he is not important dramatically or narratively.

Another opinion about this passage is that of the medieval Jewish interpreters, Gersonides and Simon ben Ẓemaḥ Duran, who say that God rebukes the friends but not Job because, even if some of Job's ideas were in error, "he spoke with sincerity throughout the dialogue."[208] Boss opines that "We can truly speak of God only if we say 'you,'" and Job *has* addressed God directly, while all the other characters only talk *about* God.[209] I also see Job's stance as sincere throughout, and his address to God as honest, and I *wish* these were the author's reasons for saying that Job spoke rightly, but I do not see the narrator openly affirming Job's sincerity. Timmer's interpretation, that the rightness is solely in Job's repentance and reverence expressed in 42:6, makes more sense in the context, although it may be less satisfying to those of us who put a high value on motives and sincerity. However, sincerity is definitely present, since the author surely understands Job's relenting in 42:6 to be sincere. This may *imply* affirmation of Job's sincerity throughout, but it is not explicitly affirmed.

Yahweh next tells the three friends to go make a large sacrifice offering, while Job will pray for them, and *then* Yahweh will show them mercy and "not to deal with you according to your folly" (42:8). Actually, a more accurate translation would be "so as not to do with you folly" (Young's Literal Translation), in other words, Yahweh was holding back from *doing* a folly to them. Other instances of "commit a folly" involve "outrageous acts."[210] The friends' sacrifices and Job's prayer are averting God from committing violence.

---

208. Eisen, *Book of Job in Medieval*, 195; and see 162.

209. Boss, *Human Consciousness*, 244–45.

210. Guillaume, "Dismantling," 497–98.

The three do what they are told, Job prays for them, and Yahweh accepts Job's prayer. This is an ironic outcome. The cocksure representatives of conventional theology had no suspicion that *they* had aroused the Lord's wrath, and that it required the good will of the rebellious-seeming Job to rescue them from punishment.

LaCocque sees great importance in Job being asked to pray for the three friends. He sees this as Yahweh making Job "an *actual* collaborator with God in correcting the wrongs committed by foolish people"; he makes Job "a kind of viceroy."[211] The retributive theology of the friends is now seen to have been arrogant. With each argument they were building up an increasingly "high opinion of themselves" and imagining themselves to be "recipients of divine rewards for their shining virtues."[212] The attempt to solve the problem intellectually leads to oppressive theology. The "book's main purpose is to reveal God as destroyer of a fundamentalist and closed-minded worldview."[213] Probably less convincing is LaCocque's argument that Yahweh is shown not to be omnipotent, rather he has to struggle against evil.[214] LaCocque sees the Elohim concept of power and justice as potentially tyrannical. What is needed is Yahweh, who is *relational*, as emphasized in Yahweh's four-time mentioning of "my servant Job."[215] LaCocque points out that it was Elohim who ordered the sacrifice of Isaac, seen to be legitimate in the eyes of ANE religion, while Yahweh's "angel stops the murderous arm of Abraham."[216] His theory is intriguing, and it attributes an interesting purpose to Yahweh's exoneration of his servant Job. I don't know, however, if I am convinced that LaCocque successfully rescues the Yahweh speeches from their bullying tone. Nor am I convinced that Job now "realizes that God

---

211. LaCocque, "Deconstruction," 94.

212. LaCocque, "Deconstruction," 95.

213. LaCocque, "Deconstruction," 96.

214. LaCocque, "Deconstruction," 96.

215. LaCocque, "Deconstruction," 97.

216. LaCocque, "Deconstruction," 96. Elohim in Genesis 22:1, 3, 9; Yahweh in 22:11.

was from the beginning on the side of the victim."[217] Guillaume's skeptical response is: "This moving Girardian statement covers up the fact that the same God allows the satan to torture Job," with the only constraint being that he could not take his life.[218] Guillaume's solution, however, is not more satisfying than LaCocque's. Guillaume says evil will continue to happen because of Yahweh's bouts of "divine folly" that oppress people; "there is a dark potential in the divine."[219] The scholars' wrestling with the meaning of the last chapters of Job reflects the ambiguity of the person of Yahweh in Job 38—42. Does Yahweh allow Job to be oppressed unjustly? Yes. Does Yahweh end up taking Job's side against the friends, and re-establish his status in society? Yes. Does Yahweh's appearance help Job to come back into good relationship with the Divine? Also yes.

In the end, the Lord restores Job's fortunes. His brothers and sisters come to him and comfort him regarding "all the evil that the Lord had brought upon him" (42:11). The Lord blesses Job, giving him the same number of sons and daughters (seven and three), but *double* the number of sheep, camels, oxen, and donkeys that he had in the Prologue (1:3), although there is no mention of servants to match the servants in 1:3. It is a happy ending. Unexpectedly, the daughters are named and are given a share of the inheritance (42:14–15), which normally only happens if there are no male heirs; the sons are not named. Vicchio thinks the daughters' marriageability is being highlighted.[220] They are the most beautiful women in the land (42:15), with appealing, sensual names. In any case, the grace that is extended to Job is also extended to his sons and daughters.

Job had demonstrated loyalty to Yahweh despite inexplicable suffering. Now, after his statement of loyalty and humility, the suffering is made to cease.

217. LaCocque, "Deconstruction," 95.

218. Guillaume, "Dismantling," 496.

219. Guillaume, "Dismantling," 499.

220. Vicchio, *Job*, 296.

The Meaning of Yahweh's Address

We saw that Rowley said that, in chapter 42, Job overcomes his "intellectual problem,"[221] that the *experience* of reconciliation with God is more satisfying than the intellectual issues Job had raised. Also favoring the experiential over the intellectual is Rudolf Otto, who says, "The *mysterium* . . . is incommensurable with thoughts of rational human teleology and is not assimilated to them: it remains in all its mystery"; but this experience is how "Job's soul [is] brought to peace."[222] The experience is beyond "anything that can be exhaustively rendered in rational concepts."[223]

In contrast to these views is the interpretation of Robert Sutherland, who offers a blunt and shocking assessment of God's hectoring questions: "At first glance, the whirlwind appears to be nothing more than a windbag . . . God's point is of limited worth. Job has never claimed omniscience."[224] The author of Job seems to be drawing upon two psalms that themselves draw upon Egyptian and Canaanite mythology, as seen in "some interesting parallels in Psalms 104 and 89 . . . 'You set the earth on its foundations . . . you water the mountains . . . There go the ships, and Leviathan that you formed to sport in it'" (Ps 104:5, 13, 26; cf. Ps 89:9–11).[225]

When it comes to Leviathan, and God's control over it, Sutherland sees the book of Job drawing upon the Canaanite myth of the conquest of the chaos monster.[226] This myth, then, is adapted by Psalm 74: "you divided the sea by your might; you broke the heads of the dragons in the waters. You crushed the heads of Leviathan"[227] (Ps 74:13–14). One of the purposes of the remarks about Leviathan, Robert Sutherland claims, is to show that evil has

---

221. Rowley, "Intellectual Versus Spiritual," 342.

222. Otto, *Idea of the Holy*, 80.

223. Otto, *Idea of the Holy*, 79.

224. Sutherland, *Putting God on Trial*, Kindle loc. 1042, 1050.

225. Sutherland, *Putting God on Trial*, Kindle loc. 1056–70.

226. Sutherland, *Putting God on Trial*, Kindle loc. 1316.

227. Sutherland, *Putting God on Trial*, Kindle loc. 1320.

always been present in the created world; it did not begin with Adam's and Eve's choices.[228]

Sutherland suggests, "The image of Leviathan carries with it two time frames: the beginning of time and the end of time. The beginning of time is the creation . . . of the chaos monster [while] the end of time is the destruction of that chaos monster and an answering of all questions."[229] He claims that, at the messianic banquet, God gives answers to humanity, while everyone devours the monster's flesh.[230] Sutherland argues that God allowed evil to enter the world at the beginning, and he will carve it up and have it devoured at the end of history. The problem is that this final slaying of Leviathan is never mentioned in Job, but only in Isaiah 27:1, while a possible final banquet occurs at Isaiah 25:6–8, and Psalm 74:14 says "You crushed the heads of Leviathan; you gave him as food for the creatures of the wilderness." Sutherland sees God promising, in Job 40–41, to answer the question of evil by slaying the monster who embodies it,[231] but this is far from clear in the text of Job. Some apocryphal works (4 Ezra 6:49–52; Apocalypse of Baruch or 2 Baruch 29:4) explicitly mention these beasts being consumed by the righteous in the messianic age.[232] Second Baruch 29:4 has Behemoth and Leviathan coming forth at the end, "and they will be nourishment for all who are left."[233] Sutherland's thesis would require that one or more of these passages, from Isaiah or Psalms or Ezra or 2 Baruch, were present in the minds of the author and readers of Job, but that the author chose not to mention the final banquet.

---

228. Adams, *Redefining Job*, 173.

229. Sutherland, *Putting God on Trial*, Kindle loc. 1486.

230. Sutherland, *Putting God on Trial*, Kindle loc. 1682.

231. Adams, *Redefining Job*, 174.

232. Pope, *Job*, 321. He gives an incorrect chapter number for the Apocalypse of Baruch. See also Vicchio, *Job*, 275–76. Rashi apparently supported the idea of their being "food for the people in the messianic age" (Boss, *Human Consciousness*, 204n10).

233. *OTP* 1:630.

As for Job repenting in "dust and ashes" (42:6), Sutherland thinks it is a further act of defiance and dispute, and not "repentance" at all. "The phrase 'dust and ashes' implies a continuation of Job's lawsuit with a certain defiance."[234] He cites Genesis 18:27, where Abraham says "I who am but dust and ashes" while challenging God to not destroy Sodom and Gomorrah if he finds forty-five righteous people there, or forty, or thirty, or twenty, or ten.[235] "Dust and ashes" is a common biblical term for a degraded or mournful state. Sutherland does not show that "dust and ashes" is associated with defiance.

Sutherland sees "God being the defendant in Job's legal Oath of Innocence. (Job 27:2–6; 31:35–37)."[236] He sees Job as winning his case against God, thus forcing God to give those answers about the final defeat of evil and the consumption of the chaos monster. He argues that, for the author, "God is the author of evil in the world. The evil is both natural and moral," citing 1:12; 2:10; 42:11.[237] God either does not or cannot create a perfect world with no evil in it, yet God does actually love his creatures, despite their imperfection.[238] This is "the particular type of love known as grace."[239]

Sutherland does not effectively prove his case; his arguments are a stretch, but they provide a valuable counterpoint to the views that see no problem with Yahweh's imperious rhetoric. He goes so far as to argue that "Man has a moral right to know the reason why God has created a world of undeserved and unremitted suffering,"[240] although that right "can be overridden or deferred" to the future.[241] Sutherland claims that the book of Job says the God *does* have a

---

234. Sutherland, *Putting God on Trial*, Kindle loc. 1567.

235. Sutherland, *Putting God on Trial*, Kindle loc. 1579.

236. Sutherland, *Putting God on Trial*, Kindle loc. 1764.

237. Sutherland, *Putting God on Trial*, Kindle loc. 1710.

238. Sutherland, *Putting God on Trial*, Kindle loc. 1722, 1735.

239. Sutherland, *Putting God on Trial*, Kindle loc. 1739.

240. Sutherland, *Putting God on Trial*, Kindle loc. 1757.

241. Sutherland, *Putting God on Trial*, Kindle loc. 1772.

duty to answer the problem of evil, and that he *will* answer it "at the Final Judgment."[242]

Intriguing though Sutherland's analysis may be, ultimately it does not convince. More convincing is Timmer's assessment that Yahweh's speeches succeed in getting Job to repent and show reverence, thus prompting Yahweh to affirm that Job has "spoken of me what is right" (42:7).

The Psychology of Yahweh

An interesting assessment of the Yahweh character from a psychological viewpoint is the daring and unorthodox analysis of Carl Jung. Jung's analysis is not theological but psychological, and he is merciless in his exposure of Yahweh's apparent insecurities. He says Yahweh is afraid of Job because of the latter's intelligent questions, and the evidence of this fear is the "cannonade of references to one's power, cleverness, courage, invincibility, etc."[243] "His thunderings at Job so completely miss the point that one cannot help but see how much he is occupied with himself . . . He is particularly sensitive on this point, because 'might' is the great argument . . . Yahweh had let himself be bamboozled by Satan. This weakness of his does not reach full consciousness."[244] In fact, the main problem with Yahweh is his unconsciousness, and "unconsciousness has an animal nature."[245] "He reacts irritably to every word that has the faintest suggestion of criticism, while he himself does not care a straw for his own moral code . . . One can submit to such a God only with fear and trembling . . . but a relationship of trust seems completely out of the question."[246]

Jung's is a fascinating and fearless critique of the book of Job from a psychological perspective, but analyzing everything as a

---

242. Sutherland, *Putting God on Trial*, Kindle loc. 1801–4.

243. Jung, "From *Answer to Job*," 315.

244. Jung, "From *Answer to Job*," 313–14.

245. Jung, "From *Answer to Job*," 318.

246. Jung, "From *Answer to Job*," 320.

psychological phenomenon is actually reductionistic. Everything, for Jung, is a question of human psychology. He does not expect to actually learn anything about God, if there even *is* a transcendent God. Jung does not doubt that there is a transcendent dimension in human psychology, and Jung himself has experienced it, but he is less clear about whether there is actually a personal God. He thought God was a mystery, and that the mystery corresponded to realities within the human psyche. He thought all the images of God, including his own, were inadequate. He considered himself a Christian, but "the Christian idea proves its vitality by a continuous evolution . . . We cannot continue to think in an antique or medieval way, when we enter the sphere of religious experience."[247] He might have agreed with the conclusion of Jeffrey Boss, who writes "to close off either the mystery or the enquiry is to mutilate oneself."[248]

Boss's psychological approach, however, is quite different from Jung's; he focuses on Job's own spiritual development and struggle. He does not ignore the theological aspect. In fact, he lays out this scenario of how Job's perception of God changes throughout the story. In the beginning, God is the Nurturer, but when the blows of Satan start to rain down, he becomes the Destroyer.[249] From chapter 3, God becomes the self-concealing God. The next stage, lasting throughout most of the Dialogue, is where "God becomes the far-off object of desire."[250] When God finally appears and Job is awed, God has become for him "the ineffable Holy One."[251] Even this is not the end. When Job is restored and his heart is content with his relationship with God again, then he experiences "God as destination."[252] In sum, "The book of Job warns us not to jump to conclusions . . . [T]heodicy can verge on cosmic chutzpah."[253] Boss is much more positive about the book

247. Jung, in Purrington, "Dr. Jung clarifies misunderstanding."

248. Boss, *Human Consciousness*, 200.

249. Boss, *Human Consciousness*, 22, 32, 241.

250. Boss, *Human Consciousness*, 43, 62, 242.

251. Boss, *Human Consciousness*, 198, 243.

252. Boss, *Human Consciousness*, 222, 244–45.

253. Boss, *Human Consciousness*, 227.

than Jung is. He sees Job undergoing a personal transformation when he becomes conscious of God as Holy,[254] finding answers that are satisfactory for his spiritual living. We looked earlier at Joo's opinion that the final speeches show that God gives out of generosity, rather than out of reward.[255] Jung misses these points, focusing only on Yahweh's domineering tone.

254. Boss, *Human Consciousness*, 215, 219.
255. Joo, "Biblical Atlas," 83.

2

Theological Debate

LISTING THE MAIN ANSWERS AND THE WAYS IN WHICH THEY DON'T SATISFY

Answer 1: God only punishes those who deserve it, or need to learn a lesson from it. This is the view of the friends and sometimes of Job, too. Much of the distress and confusion of all these characters is due to the fact that both Job and his friends hold "to a simplistic view of God's retributive justice,"[1] which assigns blame to those who suffer. Such theology results in repulsive and unfair explanations of many things that happen in the real world, like epidemics or earthquakes.

Answer 2: God is arbitrary, and sometimes pours out affliction indiscriminately and unfairly. There is no point and no benefit to being faithful to God (35:3). This is the view of Job when he is at his most despairing. This view is rejected by the friends, by Elihu, and by Job himself at other places in his speaking.

At the end of the day, the conflict in the book of Job is about whether or not the power of God is separate from justice. It raises the possibility that "God exists, but His rule is not moral. This separation is rejected by the book; the idea of God necessarily includes

---

1. Kynes and Kynes, *Wrestling with Job*, 69.

the moral idea."[2] The Elihu speeches and the Yahweh speeches both make this point, though in very different ways.

Answer 3: God will vindicate the just in the end. This seems to be the view of the book's author, since Job gets vindicated and restored in the end. It also is expressed, at various times, by Job (8:20–22), by Eliphaz (22:23), and by Elihu (36:6–11, 15). One thing that is unusual about the ending is that, even though it affirms conventional religious views, it vindicates Job. Somehow, the conventional view can tolerate the challenging questions of Job, perhaps because of the sincerity of his desire for an encounter with God, affirming that God was right to bet on Job in the first place. Nevertheless, it is interesting that Yahweh exalts Job and condemns the friends. Even the conventional view doesn't want the tedious Eliphaz and his friends to win.

Unfortunately we don't always see the just being vindicated and rescued in this lifetime.

Answer 4: There is an afterlife where the just will be rewarded, will have a chance to dialogue with God, and will have their understanding expanded. This is the view of Job in two places where he rises to this belief (14:13–17; 19:23–27). Many Jews and Christians hold this belief, although passages that support it within the book of Job are brief and infrequent. And many people are simply unsatisfied with promises about a future life. They want to see some justice in *this* lifetime.

Answer 5: God uses afflictions, along with dreams and direct revelations, to reach people and rescue them. God shows mercy and an energetic intention to save. These are the ideas that Job *hopes* are true (14:13–15), and which are emphatically affirmed by Elihu (33:16–18, 24–26; 36:6–8). Again, many people don't seem to experience these revelations or remarkable reversals.

Answer 6: This option states that it is not intellectual answers that we need, but a spiritual relationship. Job experiences a change when he encounters God. "What is the solution of the problem? . . . it is God Himself . . . [Job] has been afforded no insight into the enigmas that have tormented him, but he has seen

---

2. Kaufmann, "Job the Righteous Man," 70.

God Himself . . . (42:5) . . . God lets Himself be asked, and thus lets Himself be found. And He Himself is the answer."[3] A similar point is made by H. H. Rowley: "The wicked may have his prosperity, but the pious may have God; and in God he has far more than the other."[4]

Job gets us to ask questions about why the innocent suffer and the wicked prosper. These are problems that probably cannot be answered to our full satisfaction. We have to be content with partial answers and with a faith that seeks encouragement and relationship more than intellectual answers. Understanding will come, but it doesn't come at the beginning. We usually don't appreciate truth at the beginning anyway. Understanding only comes after long experience.

RATIONALIZING JOB

The questions that Job raises create great difficulty for the author and for the reader. How can one really answer these questions about undeserved suffering and rank injustice? Yet, one is impelled to try, because to not try would be to invite despairing attitudes. From the author of Job, to Elihu, to readers today, people have felt a need to find answers that indicate that there is some fairness in life, at least if the afterlife is included. We want to affirm that "the Almighty will not pervert justice . . . he . . . gives the afflicted their right" (34:12; 36:6). The author of the epilogue wanted to suppress the tendency to ask challenging questions such as Job's. Elihu offers views of God's merciful initiative, but he also tends to suppress Job's tendency to challenge God.

Sometimes the answers that are given seem stilted and unconvincing. The rationalizing approach of the medieval Jewish philosophers, which says that intellectual maturity rises above any and all suffering, is quite unsatisfying, especially if the suffering of others, and not just of ourselves, matters to us.

3. Ragaz, "God Himself," 129–30.
4. Rowley, "Intellectual Versus Spiritual," 127.

Although I find myself critiquing all the rationalizations about the book of Job, and all the attempts to justify God's ways both within and outside the book, I notice that I make some of these moves myself. I want to affirm, as strongly as Elihu does, that "the Almighty . . . is great in power and justice, and abundant righteousness he will not violate" (37:23). There must be answers, even if some of them are beyond our current understanding and require, in my view, an experience of the afterlife. It is not just *belief* in heaven that will help me, but the *experiences* that I will have there. Maybe I will only get some satisfaction when I actually meet someone in the afterlife who had died as a child in the Holocaust, and I *see* that person making spiritual progress with joy. It won't undo the cruelty and injustice which that person suffered as a child, but it will show that God cherishes the meaning and value in *that* person's life,[5] and validates his or her hope for eternity. God is the goal of all the pure in heart, and God honors all honest spiritual motivation. I believe—I *know*—that goodness endures, and evil does not. As the preacher Sojourner Truth said, "Goodness never had any beginning, it was from everlasting, and could never die. But evil had a beginning, and must have an end."[6] Nothing evil is eternal.

There is something of the eternal in our life here, but it is not *based* in our life here. "What is eternal and immortal in man is not the psychical or the physical element as such but the spiritual element which, acting in the other two, constitutes personality and realizes the image and likeness of God."[7]

My need to find meaning and value in life extends far beyond my own personal concerns and experiences. I need to know that God "does not withdraw his eyes from the righteous" (36:7), that God does indeed care for the widow and the orphan—and the political prisoner.

---

5. See Adams, *Horrendous Evils*, 31.

6. Painter, *Sojourner Truth*, 115; quoted in Omolade, "Faith Confronts Evil," 310.

7. Berdyaev, *Destiny of Man*, 255.

I understand both the rationalizing impulse and the need to ask questions. I seek to be sensitive to people's spiritual aspirations, hopes, and questions. The best things about both the characters Job and Elihu are not so much what they *say* as what they are *striving for*. Job is striving for God's justice and truth, and an experience of intimacy with God. Elihu is striving for recognition of God's saving intentions. How happy might both characters have been to have met the sage of Nazareth, and felt the warmth of his divine affection? How deeply might Job have found his spiritual needs being met, if he could have spoken to the man of Nazareth?

Certainly some of the rationalizing that goes on can be critiqued, but what is most important is the *striving for truth*, or faith seeking understanding, to use the traditional phrasing. In the eleventh century, Anselm of Canterbury gives us that precise phrase,[8] but he is borrowing the idea from the fifth-century thinker, Augustine, who said "believe so that you may understand."[9] Another expression of this idea was given by Pascal: "human things must be known in order to be loved; but Divine things must be loved in order to be known."[10] Knowledge of God has always been granted not necessarily to the learned or to those admired by society, "but to all those who have sought it with a true and humble heart," to those with "discernment rather than any kind of cleverness."[11] Truth comes to the "eager and simple of heart."[12]

If we are really seeking the truth of God, we are already receiving it, and we are already in the kingdom of God. It is the sincerity and purity of spiritual desire that ensures the eventual fulfillment of that desire. "Blessed are the pure in heart, for they will see God" (Matt 5:8). The honest *desire* for truth is the guarantor of its

8. He wrote "I do not seek to understand that I may believe, but I believe so that I may understand . . . unless I do believe I shall not understand" (Anselm, *Proslogion*, chapter 1, from Cannon, "Anselm's Faith").

9. Augustine, *Tractates on the Gospel of John* XXIX,6; from Barr, "St. Augustine."

10. From his *De l'esprit géométrique*, quoted in Baillie, *Interpretation of Religion*, 364–65.

11. Baillie, *Interpretation of Religion*, 365.

12. Baillie, *Interpretation of Religion*, 366.

eventual reception: "Blessed are those who hunger and thirst for righteousness, for they will be filled" (Matt 5:6).

I speak now less of the character Job, than of the readers of Job who have sought truth with a whole heart, who say to God "Teach me what I do not see" (Job 34:32). God reveals Godself to us always to the limit of our capacity for receptivity. "When you search for me, you will find me; if you seek me with all your heart, I will let you find me, says the Lord" (Jer 29:13–14).

As we live our lives, we need spiritual confidence and idealism, a desire to do God's will, and a trust in God's watchcare over us and over all creation. "Faith" is fundamentally *trust*, more than intellectual belief.[13] And trust is relational, affective. Trust is a trust *in someone*. We don't first intellectually reason our way to God. We first live with loyalty to our highest values; we cling to the reality and love of God, and *then* certain beliefs emerge from that way of living. Our ideals and faith must ever extend beyond our knowledge and understanding. Our spiritual reach will always exceed our cognitive grasp.

There is more good than we realize. God sees further than we can see. God knows where and when every good project is revisited, every good thought is revived, every good relationship is resumed. Poetically stated:

> There shall never be one lost good!
> What was, shall live as before . . .
> The high that proved too high, the heroic for earth too hard,
> The passion that left the ground to lose itself in the sky,
> Are music sent up to God by the lover and the bard;
> Enough that He heard it once: we shall hear it by and by.[14]

The problem of evil cannot be helpfully addressed without positing an afterlife where unrealized potentials get a chance to be realized, where growth is not impeded by violence, disease, or evil influences. Belief in an afterlife does not solve all possible problems. But enduring solutions can hardly even be approached

13. Faith's "primary meaning was not *credence* but rather *reliance*" (Baillie, *Interpretation of Religion*, 377).

14. Browning, "Abt Vogler," ninth and tenth stanzas; *Selected Poems*, 225.

without belief in the afterlife. Justice and fulfillment are sometimes rare in the material world; here there is an abundance of injustice and loss. Real solutions must await insights and experiences to be gained in the afterlife.

Browning's poem gives beautiful expression to the idea that noble ideas and hopes are sometimes of brief appearance on earth, like strains of music that did not take form as a finalized composition. No matter. "Enough that God heard it once"; those ideas and hopes will get a chance to be developed in the next life.

This hope was dim and embryonic in the Jewish faith, but it became a central component of the Christian faith.

DEBATE IN THE JEWISH TRADITION

In the Jewish tradition, especially but not solely in the rabbinic tradition, there is a tolerance for divergent viewpoints and theological debate. It is important to point out its presence within the pages of the Bible. For instance, "Ruth [is] a direct attack on one of the main points of the program advanced by the Ezra-Nehemiah school of thought,"[15] the rule against any kind of intermarriage. The book of Jonah is a bitingly satirical attack on common nationalistic attitudes of Israelite superiority to the nations. In this oft-misunderstood story, pagan sailors and Assyrians—and even the Assyrians' cattle!—are more cooperative with God's will than is the bigoted prophet, Jonah.[16] The sack-beclothed Assyrians and cattle may be funny, but they are not half as ridiculous as the pouting prophet who resents God's mercy upon gentiles. Jonah is a representative of reluctant Israel, wrapped up in himself and having no compassion for gentiles.[17]

There is an ongoing debate within the pages of the Bible about the appropriateness of sacrificial ritual. Whole books of the Bible

15. Orlinsky, "Nationalism-Universalism," 229–30.

16. When the Assyrian king accepts the command to repent, he decrees that all the people and even the animals shall fast and wear sackcloth (Jonah 3:7–8). God then averts his wrath, which makes Jonah angry (3:10—4:1).

17. West, "Irony in the Book of Jonah," 236.

(Exodus, Leviticus, Numbers) provide rules about sacrifice and reasons for its practice, while a number of prophets attack sacrifice (Isa 1:11–17; Jer 7:22–23; Amos 5:25; Ps 40:6), even making fun of it: "altars for sinning" (Hos 8:11; see also 4:8); "If I were hungry, I would not tell you . . . Do I eat the flesh of bulls, or drink the blood of goats?" (Ps 50:12–13; see also Mic 6:6–7).

The presentation of differing concepts of God in the book of Job is fully consistent with the Jewish tradition of allowing theological debate and disagreement, even disagreement with what is found in revered texts.

3

Possible Philosophic Answers

RESPONSES TO EVIL

Why is there evil? The philosopher Leibniz argued that evil exists in the world because God insists on allowing humans to have free will, a capacity that often leads to evil choices. This is called the free will defense, and Alvin Plantinga spells it out a little more: "A world containing creatures who are significantly free (and freely perform more good than evil actions) is more valuable . . . than a world containing no free creatures at all. Now God can create free creatures, but He can't *cause* or *determine* them to do only what is right," for then they would not be *free*.[1] To create creatures freely capable of moral good required that these creatures also be capable of moral evil. That means that sometimes things happen that are not in accord with God's will.[2]

This is fine, as far as it goes, but it doesn't answer the question: why is there *so much* evil? The free will defense is valid and essential, but it is "woefully incomplete"[3] as a comprehensive answer to the evident overabundance of evil. Some people use the problem of evil to conclude that God does not exist. Peter van Inwagen

---

1. Plantinga, "Free Will," 118.
2. Belitsos, *Truths about Evil*, 35.
3. Adams, *Redefining Job*, 178.

paraphrases their thinking thus: "If there were an omnipotent, morally perfect being who knew about these evils—well they wouldn't have arisen in the first place."[4] One way of dealing with this challenge is to conclude that God is morally perfect and good, but not omnipotent. That is Thomas Oord's conclusion.

Open and Relational Theology

Process theology emphasizes a dynamic relationship between God and the world, with each influencing the other.

Thomas Oord offers a version of process theology called open and relational theology that says God *can't* stop all evil, that God is all-loving but is not omnipotent. He argues, "It's impossible to portray a God of perfect love if we also say God could prevent genuine evil but fails to do so. A God who wants, causes, or even permits pointless pain is not a God who loves everyone."[5] Recognizing God as less than all-powerful enables one to say "God is not culpable for causing or allowing evil."[6]

Oord's theology is consistent: "God is neither omnipotent nor impotent. I recommend saying God is 'amipotent': divine power is the power of love."[7] He pictures a God who can really be loved: "God cannot leave us, cannot forsake us, always suffers with us, always empathizes, always accepts, and is essentially for creation."[8] He argues that God "everlastingly creates," and that God always creates out of love.[9] God is not controlling or domineering. God practices many kinds of love, but God does not send anyone to hell.[10] "A loving God doesn't punish and always forgives."[11]

---

4. Inwagen, "Argument," 60.

5. Oord, "Essay in Pluriform," 5.

6. Oord, "Essay in Pluriform," 5.

7. Oord, "Essay in Pluriform," 5.

8. Oord, "Essay in Pluriform," 6.

9. Oord, "Essay in Pluriform," 6–7.

10. Oord, "Essay in Pluriform," 7.

11. Oord, "Essay in Pluriform," 8.

Human Responsibility

Oord's theology is an interesting possible response to the problem of evil in the presence of a loving God. I, however, would like to affirm the idea of divine omnipotence, recognizing that God has reasons for not arbitrarily intervening on the earthly level. It is not because "God can't,"[12] but because God *doesn't*. God has reasons for not intervening. The fundamental reason seems to be that we humans have to learn through experience, and no achievement is meaningful if it is not achieved by human effort. We have to put our own house in order; God is not going to do it for us. If we want freedom and justice, we need to develop institutions that will protect those realities. If we don't want to be ruled by Hitlers, then we need a government that rules by other methods. A non-Hitlerian government is an *achievement* and an *evolved product* of decisions made and laws enacted.

I am not just arguing for human responsibility (which I am). I am also observing the necessity of human choice, effort, and achievement. None of our institutions are meaningful unless we have evolved them, used them, defended them, and reformed them. Divine intervention to establish goodness and suppress evil would not be a real human achievement, and would probably not endure, once we were left to our own devices *after* the intervention. We have to be educated enough, principled enough, and mature enough to develop progressive civilization. Thus, one of the important responses to evil is to create and maintain social institutions that work justly. We cannot undo the injustice of the past, but we can work to prevent its perpetuation in the present.

We need to become psychologically educated, so that we can recognize unhealthy undercurrents in our theology. Theodicy can often embody a quite unhealthy self-centeredness. "That many responses to the problem of evil are primarily defensive in tone makes them perfect carriers of unconscious narcissistic work."[13] It is often true that "the challenges they seek to ward off are challenges

---

12. *God Can't* is the title of a book of Oord's.
13. McClelland, "Normal Narcissism," 200.

to our narcissistic equilibrium"; and this accounts for "the mark-edly *aggressive* quality of many theodictic arguments."[14] McLelland is not using the word "narcissistic" as synonymous with "patholog-ical" or "self-aggrandizing," but rather as a function of the normal mind seeking equilibrium.[15] Nevertheless, his remarks point out the anxiety and imbalance (and aggressiveness) indicated by some theodictic arguments. And he does allow that there are some "spe-cifically pathological responses to the problem of evil."[16] McLel-land is mainly speaking about the aggressiveness and pathology manifested by theists, but I think the same observations cover the arguments of anti-theists.

I think that atheistic arguments, especially when they rail against injustice and pain, are often very narcissistically focused. These arguments manifest feelings of injury and indignation, but do not seem to really seek an answer, which would require intel-lectual humility and spiritual deepening. It takes a theistic view-point to really appreciate the drama of Job. It is radically different from much of modern literature. "The psychological orientation of so much of modern literature, indeed of modern culture, reflects the inevitable egotism of a Godless universe," which obsesses with complaining, and does not really seek God.[17] The passion in the book of Job is there because Job urgently seeks God. The reality of God drives us to seek a better world and better relationships.

THE CO-SUFFERING OF GOD

One important answer to the problem of evil is to realize that God suffers with us. "God's goodness and love include sorrow . . . This sorrow is arguably not a defect, but a strength or an asset, a part of being supremely good."[18] This is the principle expressed in Third

14. McClelland, "Normal Narcissism," 200.

15. McClelland, "Normal Narcissism," 188.

16. McClelland, "Normal Narcissism," 205.

17. Goodheart, "Job and the Modern World," 104.

18. Ekstrom, "Suffering," 104.

Isaiah: "In all their affliction he was afflicted, and the angel of his presence saved them: in his love and in his pity he redeemed them" (Isa 63:9 KJV, ASV). Alternatively, "In all their suffering, He suffered, and the Angel of His Presence saved them. He redeemed them because of His love and compassion" (HCSB). On the human level, love always involves suffering if the loved one is suffering. It is not unreasonable to expect that divine love also involves fellow-suffering. "The lover's concern for the beloved is disinterested,"[19] not selfishly motivated. Sometimes, in our human suffering, we draw near to God, including to God's suffering. Laura Waddell Ekstrom calls this "divine intimacy theodicy."[20] Not all suffering has this result, but sometimes "a certain kind of meaning *can* be found in suffering."[21] Thus, it is "a partial theodicy."[22] It may be that "the valley of suffering is the vale of soul-making."[23]

We have to accept that suffering goes with the territory, the territory of a material world, a world that is unfinished, only partially evolved. The human race is still growing up (fitfully and with plenty of resistance). There is a "long and gradual cosmic awakening to rightness," as seen in the world's great religions.[24] "Both rightness and the religious awakening to rightness, in any case, mean something new when we interpret them in the context of a universe that is still coming into being."[25]

Suffering is not a punishment, but is inherent in the nature of an imperfect and unfinished universe. Social life will also always involve suffering in an imperfect world. It is our task to work on helping to perfect it, as well as allowing ourselves, individually, to be perfected by the action of God. It is not God's job to secure a pain-free environment, but to provide a world in which

19. Ekstrom, "Suffering," 103.

20. Ekstrom, "Suffering," 96.

21. Ekstrom, "Suffering," 109.

22. Ekstrom, "Suffering," 109.

23. Wolterstorff, *Lament*, 97. The "vale of soul-making" comes from a letter by John Keats (Belitsos, *Truths about Evil*, 120).

24. Haught, *New Cosmic Story*, 27.

25. Haught, *New Cosmic Story*, 29.

people can grow spiritually. The world's "value is to be judged, not primarily by the quantity of pleasure and pain occurring in it at any particular moment, but by its fitness for its primary purpose, the purpose of soul-making."[26] We should recognize that "human goodness slowly built up through personal histories of moral effort has a value in the eyes of the Creator which justifies even the long travail of the soul-making process."[27] It is a risky and noble effort, "a hazardous adventure in individual freedom."[28]

God is not impassive and unmoved by human suffering. Classical Christian doctrine described God as impassive, perhaps largely to avoid the error of thinking that God suffered emotional swings and involuntary passions, and also to reduce the distortion of our concept of the Infinite by projecting human limitations onto God. But this thinking made God seem cold and remote, and it moves too far away from the longsuffering God of the Old Testament ("I will have pity on the house of Judah," Hos 1:7; "The Lord longs to be gracious to you," Isa 30:18 NIV). Instead, we should recognize "the love which is of its very essence capable of suffering, as the divine mercy."[29] We can hardly be satisfied with a remote, unfeeling God whose goodness is purely abstract.

If one can see God participating in one's own suffering, it changes the way one looks at suffering. "To discover in one's own pain the pain of God means finding fellowship with God in one's own suffering."[30] Of course, we should extend this insight to others, and imagine God suffering in all the suffering of others. An important aspect of this topic is the help that suffering people can offer to other sufferers. Carol Winkelmann writes about how women in a women's shelter tell their stories to each other, and often "evidence some theological reconceptualizations based on local knowledge and lived experience," moving away from individual-based

---

26. Hick, "World as a Vale," 227.

27. Hick, "World as a Vale," 225.

28. Hick, "World as a Vale," 225.

29. Moltmann, *Way of Jesus*, 179.

30. Moltmann, *Way of Jesus*, 180.

theodicies toward more socially oriented models of thinking.[31] "In short, women help women to move dialectically through the healing process."[32] Through sympathetic dialogue, these women are practicing love and experiencing healing. The best way to answer the problem of evil is to show solidarity with those who are suffering. "Salvation means coming out of evil and experiencing deliverance into a new reality."[33] Of course, it is only a partial answer, as are *all* the answers. In fact, solidarity of feeling is better than any rationalizing answer.[34] It involves "the suspension of explanation in favor of bearing one another's burdens," which "means delving deep into the common humanity that we all share and affirming that commonality together."[35]

The empathy of God is emphasized in such sayings as these: "The Lord has comforted his people, and will have compassion on his suffering ones" (Isa 49:13). "I will exult and rejoice in your steadfast love, because you have seen my affliction" (Ps 31:7). The Hebrew word for compassion, *rāḥam*, is derived from the word for "womb" or "uterus," signifying deep and tender love, as of a mother.[36]

THE COMPASSION OF JESUS

Although it takes us beyond the scope of the book of Job, the issue of compassion cannot help but turn our thinking toward Jesus, which opens up a realm of reflection on the theme of suffering. After reflecting on compassion in the Old Testament, Sharon Baker says, "We see that same kind of loving compassion in Jesus as he sits weeping on the Mount of Olives, looking over the city

---

31. Winkelmann, "'In the Bible,'" 165.

32. Winkelmann, "'In the Bible,'" 166.

33. Winkelmann, "'In the Bible,'" 179.

34. See Castelo, *Theological Theodicy*, 94.

35. Castelo, *Theological Theodicy*, 99.

36. Baker, *Razing Hell*, 74.

of Jerusalem."[37] Pope John Paul II wrote, "Christ is *proof of God's solidarity with man in his suffering*."[38] Incidentally, one does not need to believe in the penal substitutionary or the vicarious merit theories of atonement, nor in original sin, in order to accept that statement. I do not believe in those theories, but I *do* believe in the Divine incarnation of the Son, and am moved by the Son's many expressions of fellow-feeling during his life, even unto death on a cross. In Jesus' life, the Divine suffered as a human being, and showed solidarity with humanity. Notice how Jesus goes out of his way to serve the little people, the suffering, how he stops his preaching to minister to a group of people who tore apart the roof over his head in order to draw close to him (Mark 2:3–5). Even when performing miracles, he shows his very human pity and affection. In his life, we learn about God's kindness and openness to gentiles, to children, to crippled and sick people, to widows, and even to tax collectors, who were wealthy but were looked down upon by others. Jesus had compassion on the crowds "because they were harassed and helpless" (Matt 9:36; see also Matt 14:14; 15:32; Mark 6:34; 8:2).

Hebrews says that it was a necessity of Jesus' human incarnation that he had to "share flesh and blood" with us, that "he had to become like his brothers and sisters in every respect" (Heb 2:14, 17). This is the experiential basis for his compassion. Hebrews says, "Because he himself was tested by what he suffered, he is able to help those who are being tested" (2:18). And because he was been tested, he is able "to sympathize with our weaknesses" (Heb 4:15). I quote these lines without quoting the atonement theology that surrounds them in order to affirm the concept of Jesus suffering and sharing the human lot, without adding any notion of substitutionary pay-off. The suffering was not a payment. It was a deep participation in human life. It was *living and suffering as we live and suffer*.

37. Baker, *Razing Hell*, 74.

38. Pope John Paul II, *Crossing the Threshold*, 63; quoted in Echeverria, "Redemptive Suffering," 126.

Life tests us constantly, doesn't it? Too much, in fact! We wish it would stop. Enough with the testing! The constant testing can wear us out! Who sees this, who recognizes that we are feeling the pressure of life? Jesus does. He knows the tediousness of being constantly misunderstood, even by one's closest friends and family. He knows the fatigue of doing one's best, and it never being enough.

Eduardo Echeverria reflects that "the individual discovers Christ himself as the personal answer to the problem of suffering ... For him, evil and suffering are not irreconcilable with God's goodness and power; rather they have become an indispensable element in God's providential plan."[39] This suffering should make one compassionate about the suffering of others.[40] We can affirm that the Divine, through Jesus, experienced human suffering, and that this is evidence of divine compassion.

Jesus exercised steadfast love throughout his life. Given the form it took at the end of his earth life, and given the multicultural fact of sacrifice, it was probably inevitable that some sacrificial mysticism got drawn into the interpretations of his life and death. But we do not *need* to add any mysticism about sacrificial suffering as a magical purchase of salvation. That would be to perpetuate an old mythology where sacrifice is a kind of magical payment. Rather, I am happy to affirm Hosea's "I desire steadfast love and not sacrifice" (6:6), twice quoted by Jesus himself (Matt 9:13; 12:7). The point of the incarnation was solidarity, not substitutionary payment.

Jürgen Moltmann correctly argues that the New Testament does not present the Son as expiating the Father. Rather, "the Father of Jesus Christ is always on Jesus' side, never on the side of the people who crucified him ... [T]he giving up of the Son reveals the giving up of the Father. In the suffering of the Son, the pain of the Father finds a voice."[41] To believe that Jesus appeased God, or that God acted "through Judas, Caiaphas, Pilate, and his torturers"

---

39. Echeverria, "Redemptive Suffering," 145.

40. Echeverria, "Redemptive Suffering," 146.

41. Moltmann, *Way of Jesus*, 176.

would be inappropriately to divide Jesus from God.[42] Rather, "*God himself was in Christ* (II Cor. 5.19) . . . Jesus' suffering was God's suffering."[43] This is "the theology of *the divine co-suffering or compassion.*"[44] "Christ too was murdered in Auschwitz."[45] "In Christ God joins Godself to the hurting and the dying . . . The incarnation shows that humans are not alone, that God has not abandoned the creation."[46]

Jesus' empathy is real and experience-based. He understands us; he knows what we go through. He drank the cup of human experience, draining it to the bottom. He had to put up with incomprehension from his immediate family, who so misunderstood him that they thought he was beside himself, and "they went out to restrain him" (Mark 3:21). But he had patience with his family, and (after the resurrection) they came around to believing in him. He also had to practice patience with his often uncomprehending apostles. The Son is able "to sympathize with our weaknesses" (Heb 4:15).

The truths that Jesus uttered were sometimes timeless truths, like "the truth will make you free" (John 8:32), and sometimes were truths wrung out of the sweat and blood of painful experience, such as that "prophets are not without honor, except in their home town, and among their own kin, and in their own house" (Mark 6:4). Those who hold these ideas are inclined toward compassion for those who suffer. "Anyone who believes in the forgiveness of sins begins to weep over the injustice of this world, and waits for the wiping away of tears which only this forgiveness of sins can and must complete . . . The individual does not believe and love, hope and weep for himself, but for other people."[47] Job shows an interest in the suffering of others in 21:7; 24:2–16, 21. Elihu seems to want to rescue Job from suffering (33:16–33; 36:5–16).

42. Moltmann, *Way of Jesus*, 176.

43. Moltmann, *Way of Jesus*, 177.

44. Moltmann, *Way of Jesus*, 178.

45. Moltmann, *Way of Jesus*, 210.

46. Castelo, *Theological Theodicy*, 86.

47. Moltmann, *Way of Jesus*, 193.

The concept of the incarnation can change our view about the relationship between God and humanity. It can also alert us to the movement of the Divine into human life, and motivate us to assist in that process. "It is bearing fruit and growing in the whole world" (Col 1:6). Teilhard de Chardin saw God as penetrating, through the incarnation, into nature and into human nature: "By the Incarnation God descended into nature to 'super-animate' it and lead it back to Him."[48] Teilhard saw Christ as deeply involved in the human race and in its painful evolutionary struggles, directing it toward a spiritual goal. Teilhard spoke of "Christ-Omega: the Christ, therefore, who animates and gathers up all the biological and spiritual energies developed by the Universe. Finally, then, Christ the evolver."[49] He says Christ is gradually guiding and nudging humanity toward a spiritual destiny. "By virtue of the penetration of the Divine into our nature, a new life was born . . . The Incarnation is a renewal and restoration of all the forces and powers of the universe . . . *The mystical Christ has not yet attained His full growth* . . . He will consummate the universal unification."[50] Teilhard quotes Ephesians 4:10 to make his point: "'He descended, and he ascended, that he might fill all things'—there you have the very economy of the incarnation."[51]

Theology about the incarnation of the Divine Son was completely unavailable to the authors of Job, who did the best they could with the concepts that were available. The argumentation in Job might have gone quite differently if there had been the concept of a divine Son living a human life and experiencing suffering. But even the Isaian concept of God suffering in all our sufferings (63:9) was apparently unknown to the authors of Job.

Yet Job is a worthy and engaging work that compels us to think. And I think we can be inspired by what Job strives for (a true assessment and vindication by God) and what Elihu strives for (a

---

48. Teilhard de Chardin, *Human Energy*, 178.

49. Teilhard de Chardin, *Let Me Explain*, 102. Original source: *Science and Christ*.

50. Teilhard de Chardin, *Future*, 304–5, 308.

51. Teilhard de Chardin, *Toward*, 106.

recognition of God's merciful efforts to save and instruct people). What we strive for is more spiritually significant than what we have achieved. What we are reaching for is more important than where we are at. Our aspirations have a prophetic-eschatological value, signaling the way forward into the undisclosed future, even the future when "God may be all in all" (1 Cor 15:28).

Finally, I would say that we can more fully appreciate the contribution of the book of Job if we have a concept of the progressive development and advance of religious insight over time. We don't expect Job to say the things that the Gospels would say. But we can appreciate the book for its insights into the mercy and love of God. Like the Psalms, it manifests a wide range of personal expressions of piety, faith, doubt, suffering, and perseverance. Both works affirm, "The Lord has heard my supplication; the Lord accepts my prayer" (Ps 6:9). Further expressions of faith and truth will come with the great prophets, and then with the Gospels.

With these ideas about struggle and progress in mind, I hope the reader can appreciate my effort in the stage play that follows.

Appendix

A Stage Play:
The Questions of Job

The story of the book of Job, with a peak behind the curtain. Characters, in order of appearance:

Narrator (Voice from the wings)

Job

Job's wife

Eliphaz the Temanite

Bildad the Shuhite

Zophar the Naamathite

Elihu

Yahweh (Voice from the wings)

NARRATOR: There was a man in the land of Uz whose name was Job.

That man was perfect and upright, fearing God and rejecting evil.

He had seven sons, three daughters, seven thousand sheep, three thousand camels, five hundred she-asses, and many servants.

One day, a band of Sabeans came into his fields and slew all his sons, daughters, most of the servants, carried away the beasts, and put the fields to the torch.

When Job heard of this he tore his mantle, shaved his head, fell upon the ground, and worshipped.

JOB: Naked came I out of the womb, and naked shall I return.
> The Lord gave and the Lord has taken away.
> Blessed be the name of the Lord.

NARRATOR: Now, some say that God was testing Job's faith as an answer to the challenge of the satan, who had snarled "Doesn't Job have good reason to be faithful? Just take away his wealth and he will curse you to your face."

And so, the story goes, Yahweh—that is, God—allowed the satan to afflict Job, even to make him break out in boils from head to foot.

JOB'S WIFE: Do you still have faith, you fool? Curse God, and die!

JOB: What? Shall we receive good from the hand of God, and not receive evil?

NARRATOR: Now Job had three friends who heard of his calamity, and they came to sit with him: Eliphaz the Temanite, Bildad the Shuhite, and Zophar the Naamathite.

[*These three characters enter the stage in the order named, and sit down facing Job.*]

JOB: Let the day perish wherein I was born! Why did I not die in the womb?
> My roarings pour out like waters; I am drowned in affliction.
> Oh, that my grief were weighed in the balance, for it would be heavier than the sands of the sea!

ELIPHAZ: Will you let us talk with you?
> Once you schooled others and strengthened the weak, but now that it has come upon you, you faint!

Think now! What innocent person ever suffered?

Those who *plant* wickedness are the ones who *reap* wickedness.

Wrath kills the foolish man, and envy kills the silly one.

But God saves the reverent man.

Happy is he whom the Lord corrects, for the hand that hurts is also the hand that heals.

JOB: Aren't my days almost over? Let me have a moment's peace before I go to the place of no return, the land of murk and deep shadow.

He that goes down to the grave shall come up no more; isn't that what they say?

But where have I erred? There is no lie on my tongue! But I have to speak the anguish of my spirit.

Why do the wicked still live on, their power increasing with their age? God does not punish them. Their tents are left in peace.

This state of affairs is all God's fault!

BILDAD: Is there no end to your blustering? Why do you wail like the wind?

Does God pervert justice?

If you pray to the Almighty, he will awake for you and make you prosperous.

This is all *your* fault.

JOB: Is that true? I was in peace, but he dislodged me, and handed me over to the wicked. He set me up for target; his arrows strike me from all directions, even though my hands are free from violence, and my prayer is sincere.

Do not silence my cry! I will speak my mind before God, come what may. I take my life in my hands. Though he slay me, yet will I trust him, but still will I defend my ways to his face!

God, tell me what charges you bring against me! Does it please you to oppress me while you smile on the schemes of the wicked?

Your hands shaped me. Will you now turn and destroy me? Did you not clothe me with skin and flesh, and knit me with bones and sinews?

Why do you hide your face and treat me as an enemy? Will you harass me as a wind-driven leaf?

Oh, but how can a mortal argue with God? His wisdom is profound, his power unlimited. How can I dispute with him? Who would issue him a summons?

I don't care any more! I despise my life. It is all the same anyway; he destroys both the blameless and the wicked. Since I am already found guilty, why should I struggle? Would that there were an arbitrator between us, who could withdraw his punishment from me.

ZOPHAR: Are all these words to go unanswered? You say you are flawless?

Oh, that God would require of you twofold for your guilt!

Can you penetrate the designs of God? How dare you vie with perfection? It is higher than the heavens—what can you do? It is deeper than the nether world—what can you know?

But if you set your heart aright, if you let no injustice dwell in your tent, then you may lift up your face in innocence, and he will withdraw your misery.

JOB: No doubt you are intelligent people—wisdom will die with you!

But I have intelligence as well. Who has not heard your platitudes? You offer only vain remedies, moldy maxims.

Man, born of woman, is short-lived and full of trouble. Like a flower that springs up and fades, he passes away. For a tree there is hope, if it be cut down, that it will sprout again. But when a man dies, then where is he?

[Looking up:] Oh, that you would hide me in the grave and keep me sheltered till your wrath is past, that you would fix a time, and then remember me!

A man has died, but he will live again. I will wait all the days of my sleep, until my change shall come.

You will call and I will answer, for you will long to see the work of your hands. Surely then you will guide my steps, and not keep watch for sin in me.

[*Another figure, Elihu, comes onto the stage, but stays in the background.*]

ELIPHAZ: Are you privy to the counsels of God? What do you know that we do not?

I say the wicked man is in torment all his days. The sound of terrors is in his ears; when all is well, the destroyer comes upon him. Isn't this what happened to you?

JOB: I have heard this sort of thing many times. What rotten comfort you offer!

I could talk as you do, if our places were reversed. But my witness is in heaven. You have wronged me, but God will do justice for a mortal.

My friends are strangers. My wife despises my breath. My bones cling to my skin, and I have escaped by the skin of my teeth!

Oh that my words were written down! That they were inscribed in a book, preserved in rock!

As for me, I know that my Redeemer lives, and that he will at last stand up, and after my body has been destroyed, yet shall I see God! I shall see; my eyes shall behold him!

But why, in this life, do the wicked prosper? Why are their houses safe from fear, and they say to God "why should we pray to you?"

BILDAD: Now you are going to be judged. Isn't your wickedness great? That is why traps surround you, and fear troubles you.

But if you receive God's words from his mouth, then you shall have gold and silver, and the Almighty will protect your investments.

JOB: Oh, that I knew where to find him! I would argue my cause before him and he would answer. When he has tried me, I shall come forth as gold.

But where is he? By his spirit he garnished the heavens, and set the boundaries of the seas, and yet how little we know of him!

And yet, as God lives, I know that I am innocent. My tongue does not utter deceit; my heart does not reproach me.

But what inheritance do we have from the Almighty?

If only God would answer me!

ELIHU: I have listened to all of you, and I cannot hold my peace. I thought "I am young and they are old; age should speak, and the multitude of years be heard."

But age does not always give wisdom. Rather, it is the spirit of God in a person, the inspiration of the Almighty, that gives one understanding. And I am ready to burst, for the spirit moves me to reply.

Job, I will not be heavy-handed with you. But why do you say that God is counting you as an enemy? Don't you see that, if indeed you have done anything wrong, God is eager to forgive?

God keeps a man's soul from going down into the pit. For there is an angel on your side as your helper, one among a thousand angels, to remind you of your duty, and to say "Deliver him from the pit, for I have discovered his redeeming qualities."

For if anyone says "I have sinned," God will deliver his soul, and he shall see the Light. God wishes to enlighten us!

If you say "lead me aright," do you think God would reject you? Would the Almighty nurse a grudge? No! He is greater than that! He is infinite, and he opens up eternity for us. Ultimate justice is there with him. Meditate on this, and do not lose faith.

You have wondered if God hears you. Of course he does! He even prompts some of your thoughts. Your moments of faith are evidence that he lives in you. Though you cannot see him, you can sense him, and your spirit tells you to trust him.

ZOPHAR: Don't listen to him, Job, he'll just get you in more trouble.

JOB [mulling it over, turns to Elihu:] On what authority do you make these daring statements about God?

ELIHU: On what authority did you cry out "My Redeemer lives!"? On what authority do you have an innate sense of justice which feels outrage not just that you should suffer, but that *any* good person should undergo terrible suffering?

On what authority does anyone question *any* idea? On the authority of an intelligent mind and the promptings of an inner witness. On the authority of the spirit of God within you!

God did not make us stupid; he gives to every person a spirit-essence of himself, so that we may begin to learn of him intimately, so that we may be his children, capable of growing spiritually, even of seeking perfection.

Did God create you to humiliate you? Or to spiritualize you?

JOB: Your words are fire within me. Part of me wants to stand up beside you and shout about the reality of a God of Justice, even . . . maybe . . . a God of Love.

But then the other part of me looks down at my sore-ridden body, and the ashes of my children's homes, and tells me to be silent, and to fear the God of Power.

[*There is a sudden whirlwind, a flash of fire, and voice from the wings:*]

YAHWEH: That's right! Where were you when I established the pillars of the earth? When the Morning Stars sang together, and the Sons of God shouted for joy? Do you know the place where light comes from? Do you know the secret of thunder? Did you give feathers to the peacock? Strength to the horse?

Behold Behemoth! I made him, with his muscles like brass, his bones like iron. How dare you speak in my presence?

ELIHU: Excuse me, but I don't think we have to take that from you.

YAHWEH: Who is this that darkens counsel with ignorant words? Give me one good reason why I shouldn't blast you for that remark.

ELIHU: Because you aren't God, or at least, the complete God. Oh sure, you represent absoluteness, but you are an early stage in the development of the God-idea. Elijah knew better when he spoke of God contacting him with "a still, small voice." That's more true than thinking of God issuing put-downs from a whirlwind. Why, even poor Job has voiced higher and truer God-concepts than *you* represent.

[turning to Job:]

Come on, speak up! This heavy-handed Deity is the one you've been rebelling against throughout this story.

JOB: My mouth is shut.

YAHWEH: Yes, you better fear me! You elders: what say you to this upstart Elihu?

ELIPHAZ: A lump of presumptuous gumption!

BILDAD: A slurring cur from Ur.

ZOPHAR: Ganz meshugge!

YAHWEH: You hear that, upstart? Maybe I should tell them to inflict a little wrath-of-God on you. Where do you get off, mister? You're not even supposed to be talking. Don't you know I'm supposed to have the last word? How can I be out-argued by somebody who doesn't even fit into the plot?

ELIHU: Just be grateful you were allowed the last word in the final version of the book of Job. You say I don't fit into the plot, but I *do* fit into the book's history. The book of Job descends from ancient Mesopotamian wisdom literature—a simple tale of suffering and restoration that was transformed into a great religious drama by Jewish sages.

I am not much of a dramatist, that is true. I wrote myself into the story because I urgently needed to inject some spiritual truth into the debate. In my time, the God of the Hebrews was a rather stormy character who sends evil as well as good, and who even could be manipulated by the satan. Job and his friends alike held to these ideas.

But *somebody* had to say something about the mercy of God, and *somebody* had to speak of God's spirit sent to dwell within people's hearts, so as to save them. There were no prophets at the time to carry the torch of truth, so I grasped it.

The dialogues of Job dramatize the conflicts that went on among monotheists in the pre-exilic period. When I encountered the book of Job, a conservative author had allowed the God-of-Lightning-and-Thunder to have the last word. But readers throughout the ages have preferred the questions of Job to the imperious attitude of this version of Yahweh.

I had to write myself into the story, so that someone might be heard to speak of God's merciful intention to reach us and save us.

I challenged the primitive idea of Yahweh that the friends advocated, and that was suffocating Job and causing him such misery.

YAHWEH (sarcastically): And were you around when the pillars of the earth were laid?

ELIHU: Of course not, I was just a twinkling in the eye of God at that time, but so were you! You only came to exist as one stage in the long evolution of the God-concept.

And you have been left behind.

If only I can get Job to speak up, we might get the last word in this play.

JOB: I'm better at soliloquy than philosophy, friend. I don't know what to make of the idea that the God about whom I've always been taught could be superseded.

YAHWEH: We'll see who gets superseded! Humble yourselves!

[*The elders tremble, and Job prostrates himself face down on the ground.*]

JOB: I am vile. I am the dirt under the fingernail of a gnat. I am—

ELIHU: Not so fast. Let's distinguish between humility and hu-miliation; between the idea of an *infinite* God and the idea of an *infinitely remote* God. You, in the wings—answer me, quickly! Is there love in your nature?

YAHWEH: Uh, well—*sure* . . . for those who fear me, and who are humble.

ELIHU: Alright, I'd say Job is more or less humble, even if he in-dulges in a presumptuous outburst or two. He's got reason, no? Do you expect him to be a placid sufferer with no passion for justice or understanding?

This guy is no scrawny ascetic. There's virility in his soul. And isn't his courage, in fact, a reflection of the values for which you stand?

YAHWEH: You could say that . . . But you *shouldn't*. You should let *me* say it! Anyway, don't I restore Job's health and wealth in the end?

ELIHU: Yes, but even your generosity is accompanied by a put-down. You discount every one of his challenges because you are not equal to the task of answering the problem of evil. There are more valid answers in Job's questions than in your answers.

What do you say, Job—are you going to allow this chest-thumping deity to force you to squelch your yearning for justice? Or are you going to dare to follow your inner light wherever it may shine—even if it leads to a greater God . . . a greater *idea* of God, that is?

[*Job stands up, looks at Elihu, looks at the wings, looks up, closes his eyes, and prays intensely.*]

JOB: God—*real* God, God beyond what anyone says about you—I pray to you now. Dare I speak out? Have you encouraged these thoughts in my heart, or were they mere presumption? Can I be-lieve in you, and still to mine own heart be true?

Will you show me the truth—either with an inner certainty that I cannot deny, or with an external trumpeting that cannot be challenged? And how will I know? Already I have heard my inner voice say one thing, and the voice of religious tradition, *another* thing.

I can't stand this uncertainty! I demand to know the truth!

[*Opening his eyes, and looking to the wings.*]

JOB: You! Speak and tell me: are you God?

[*Silence.*]

ELIHU [*standing*]: He's gone, Job. You've done it. He was just a concept derived from the beliefs of these three and, yes, from *your* beliefs, too. But you have transcended that level now. You have prayed in spirit and in truth, and now you have an inner certainty, although your mind isn't as certain as your soul is.

JOB: How many different people am I?

ELIHU: Just one, though with enough inner conflict for a dozen. But you never wholly laid down and gave in to the pressures of dogma. You took a risk by listening to me—

ELIPHAZ: Just wait till the congregation hears the things these two have been saying.

ELIHU [*to Job*]:—but you listened to a still, small and powerful voice within you, long before you listened to me.
[*Turning to the three friends:*] Hear me, you minions of mediocrity, you theocrats of thoughtless conformity to received opinion: Job hears a different drummer, whose beat is closer to the true spirit-rhythms than are yours. Oh sure, he shows an excess of exasperation. But the solution to that is not for him to stifle his inner promptings, but to cultivate them. God is not a bossy patriarch sending down bolts to make us shut up.
Job, pray and do your best. Trust that God will give you answers, not all at once, but with time. The spirit of God within you

is the promise not only of getting answers, but of your growing toward God. There is something divine in you, or you could *know nothing of God*!

BILDAD: Now they've got pieces of God in them! At the rate they're going, they'll soon be glowing.

ELIPHAZ *[nervously]*: Then comes the whirlwind—

ZOPHAR: And the fire—

[*The three look at each other.*]

ZOPHAR: Maybe we should get out of here.

BILDAD: I think I have to milk my cattle.

ELIPHAZ: I just remembered I have another pillaged and boil-ridden neighbor I need to visit.

[*They slink away, but BILDAD scampers back and says in a stage whisper:*]

BILDAD: If you two do any praying, put in a good word for me, will you?

[*JOB and ELIHU laugh, as BILDAD leaves.*]

JOB: Where would a fellah be without friends, eh? Why suffer alone when you can be berated by men like those?

ELIHU: You know, it's too bad this part didn't get into the Bible.

JOB: Yes, but it's all there between the lines. You're right, I should have had the faith to assert that God's justice is unassailable, even if there is injustice on earth. I shouldn't have retreated so quickly after each outburst of faith. Too bad the Bible readers of later times won't get to see me attain this level of satisfaction.

ELIHU: But they just might be able to discover it for themselves if, while they read the Bible, they also read God's writing in their own souls.

Bibliography

Adams, Marilyn McCord. *Horrendous Evils and the Goodness of God*. Cornell Studies in the Philosophy of Religion. Ithaca, NY: Cornell University Press, 1999.

Adams, Victoria. *Redefining Job and the Conundrum of Suffering*. Eugene, OR: Wipf and Stock, 2020.

Andersen, Francis I. *Job: An Introduction and Commentary*. Tyndale Old Testament Commentaries 14. Downers Grove, IL: InterVarsity, 1976; reprinted with new pagination in 2008.

Anderson, Bradford A. "Edom's (Dis)Possession." *CBQ* 84 (2022) 365–84.

Baillie, John. *The Interpretation of Religion: An Introductory Study of Theological Principles*. New York: Charles Scribner's Sons, 1941.

Baker, Sharon L. *Razing Hell: Rethinking Everything You've Been Taught about God's Wrath and Judgment*. Louisville: Westminster John Knox, 2010.

Barr, Stephen M. "St. Augustine and the Beginning of Time." Society of Catholic Scientists, January 30, 2020. https://catholicscientists.org/articles/st-augustine-beginning-of-time/.

Belitsos, Byron. *Truths about Evil, Sin, and the Demonic: Toward an Integral Theodicy for the Twenty-First Century*. Eugene, OR: Wipf and Stock, 2023.

Berdyaev, Nicolas. *The Destiny of Man*. Translated by Natalie Duddington. New York: Harper & Row, 1960. English original: London: Geoffrey Bles, 1955.

Boss, Jeffrey. *Human Consciousness of God in the Book of Job: A Theological and Psychological Commentary*. New York: Continuum, 2010.

Brown, Francis, S. R. Driver, and Charles A. Briggs. *The New Brown, Driver, and Briggs Hebrew and English Lexicon of the Old Testament*. Lafayette, IN: Associated Publishers and Authors, 1907; reprinted 1981.

Browning, Robert. *Selected Poems*. Harmondsworth, Middlesex, England: Penguin, 1938.

Brueggemann, Walter, and Tod Linafelt. *An Introduction to the Old Testament: The Canon and Christian Imagination*. 2nd ed. Louisville: Westminster John Knox, 2012.

Cannon, Dale. "Anselm's Faith Seeking Understanding." https://human.libretexts.org/Bookshelves/Religious_Studies/Six_Ways_of_Being_Religious_

Bibliography

(Cannon)/10%3A_The_Way_of_Reasoned_Inquiry/10.02%3A_Anselm's_Faith_Seeeking.

Castelo, Daniel. *Theological Theodicy*. Cascade Companions. Eugene, OR: Cascade, 2012.

Charlesworth, James H., editor. *The Old Testament Pseudepigrapha, Volume 1: Apocalyptic Literature and Testaments*. New York: Doubleday, 1983.

Clines, David J. A. *Job 1–20*. WBC 17. Dallas: Word, 1989.

———. *Job 21–37*. WBC 18A. Nashville: Nelson, 2006.

Crenshaw, James L. *Old Testament Wisdom: An Introduction*. Atlanta: John Knox, 1981.

Dahood, Mitchell. *Psalms II, 51–100*. Anchor Bible 17. New York: Doubleday, 1968.

Dhorme, E. *A Commentary on the Book of Job*. Translated by Harold Knight. Nashville: Nelson, 1984. Originally, Paris: Librairie Victor Lecoffre, 1926.

Driver, S. R. *The Book of Job in the Revised Version*. Oxford: Clarendon, 1906.

Echeverria, Eduardo J. "The Gospel of Redemptive Suffering: Reflections on John Paul II's *Salvifici Doloris*." In *Christian Faith and the Problem of Evil*, edited by Peter van Inwagen, 111–47. Grand Rapids: Eerdmans, 2004.

Eisen, Robert. *The Book of Job in Medieval Jewish Philosophy*. Oxford: Oxford University Press, 2004.

Ekstrom, Laura Waddell. "Suffering as Religious Experience." In *Christian Faith and the Problem of Evil*, edited by Peter van Inwagen, 95–110. Grand Rapids: Eerdmans, 2004.

Erickson, Amy. "'Without My Flesh I Will See God': Job's Rhetoric of the Body." *JBL* 132 (2013) 295–313.

Fishbane, Michael. "The Book of Job and Inner-Biblical Discourse." In *The Voice from the Whirlwind: Interpreting the Book of Job*, edited by Leo G. Perdue and W. Clark Gilpin, 86–98. Nashville: Abingdon, 1992.

Good, Edwin M. *In Turns of Tempest: A Reading of Job*. Palo Alto, CA: Stanford University Press, 1990.

———. *Irony in the Old Testament*. Philadelphia: Westminster, 1965.

Goodheart, Eugene. "Job and the Modern World." In *Twentieth Century Interpretations of the Book of Job: A Collection of Critical Essays*, edited by Paul S. Sanders, 98–106. Englewood Cliffs, NJ: Prentice-Hall, 1968.

Gordis, Robert. *The Book of God and Man: A Study of Job*. Chicago: University of Chicago Press, 1965.

Guillaume, Philippe. "Dismantling the Deconstruction of Job." *JBL* 127 (2008) 491–99.

Hartley, John E. *The Book of Job*. NICOT. Grand Rapids: Eerdmans, 1988.

Haught, John F. *The New Cosmic Story: Inside Our Awakening Universe*. New Haven: Yale University Press, 2017.

Hays, Christopher. "'There Is Hope for a Tree': Job's Hope for the Afterlife in the Light of Egyptian Tree Imagery." *CBQ* 77 (2015) 42–68.

Hick, John. "The World as a Vale of Soul-Making." In *The Problem of Evil: Selected Readings*, edited by Michael L. Peterson, 215–30. Library of

Religious Philosophy 8. Notre Dame: University of Notre Dame Press, 1992.

Höffding, Harald. *The Philosophy of Religion*. London: Macmillan, 1906.

Holladay, William L. *A Concise Hebrew and Aramaic Lexicon of the Old Testament*. Grand Rapids: Eerdmans, 1988.

Inwagen, Peter van. "The Argument from Evil." In *Christian Faith and the Problem of Evil*, edited by Peter van Inwagen, 55–73. Grand Rapids: Eerdmans, 2004.

Janzen, J. Gerald. "Blessing and Justice in Job: In/commensurable?" In *When the Morning Stars Sang: Essays in Honor of Choon Leong Seow on the Occasion of His Sixty-Fifth Birthday*, edited by Scott C. Jones and Christine Roy, 51–70. Berlin: deGruyter, 2017.

———. *Job*. Interpretation. Atlanta: John Knox, 1985.

John Paul II. *Crossing the Threshold of Hope*. New York: Knopf, 1994.

Joo, Samantha. "Job, the Biblical Atlas." *CBQ* 74 (2012) 67–83.

Jung, Carl Gustav. "From *Answer to Job*." In *The Essential Jung: Selected Writings*, selected and introduced by Anthony Storr, 310–29 and 343–45. Princeton: Princeton University Press, 1983.

Purrington, Mr. "Dr. Jung clarifies misunderstanding of BBC Broadcast of: 'I don't believe. I Know.'" Carl Jung Depth Psychology, June 30, 2020. carljungdepthpsychologysite.blog/2020/06/03/believe/#.XteLNTiHiQA. blogger.

Kaufmann, U. Milo. "Expostulation with the Divine: A Note on Contrasting Attitudes in Greek and Hebrew Piety." In *Twentieth Century Interpretations of the Book of Job: A Collection of Critical Essays*, edited by Paul S. Sanders, 65–70. Englewood Cliffs, NJ: Prentice-Hall, 1968.

Kaufmann, Yehezkel. "Job the Righteous Man and Job the Sage." In *The Dimensions of Job: A Study and Selected Readings*, edited by Nahum N. Glatzer, 65–70. Eugene, OR: Wipf and Stock, 2002. Original source: Kaufmann, *The Religion of Israel* (Chicago: University of Chicago Press, 1960), 334–38.

———. *The Religion of Israel, from Its Beginnings to the Babylonian Exile*. London: Allen & Unwin, 1961.

Kynes, Bill, and Will Kynes. *Wrestling with Job: Defiant Faith in the Face of Suffering*. Downers Grove, IL: InterVarsity, 2022.

LaCocque, André. "The Deconstruction of Job's Fundamentalism." *JBL* 126 (2007) 83–97.

Margulies, Zachary. "Oh That One Would Hear Me! The Dialogue of Job, Unanswered." *CBQ* 82 (2020) 582–604.

McClelland, Richard T. "Normal Narcissism and the Need for Theodicy." In *Christian Faith and the Problem of Evil*, edited by Peter van Inwagen, 185–206. Grand Rapids: Eerdmans, 2004.

McGrew, Israel. "'What is Enosh?' The Anthropological Contributions of Job 7:17–18 through Allusion and Intertextuality." *CBQ* 84 (2022) 404–23.

Bibliography

Moberly, R. Walter L. *The Bible, Theology, and Faith: A Study of Abraham and Jesus*. Cambridge: Cambridge University Press, 2000.

Moltmann, Jürgen. *The Way of Jesus Christ: Christology in Messianic Dimensions*. Translated by Margaret Kohl. Minneapolis: Fortress, 1993. Original: Munich: Christian Kaiser Verlag, 1989.

Moore, Michael S. *Retribution or Reality? A Short Theological Introduction to the Book of Job*. Eugene, OR: Pickwick, 2023.

Newsom, Carol A. *The Book of Job: A Contest of Moral Imaginations*. Oxford: Oxford University Press, 2003.

———. "Job." In *New Interpreter's Bible; vol. IV*, 317–637. Nashville: Abingdon, 1994.

———. "Job and His Friends." In *Interpretation* 53 (1999) 235–53.

Oesterley, W. O. E., and T. H. Robinson. "The Three Stages of the Book." In *The Dimensions of Job: A Study and Selected Readings*, edited by Nahum N. Glatzer, 214–17. Eugene, OR: Wipf and Stock, 2002. Original source: *An Introduction to the Books of the Old Testament* (London: SPCK, 1934).

Omolade, Barbara. "Faith Confronts Evil." In *Christian Faith and the Problem of Evil*, edited by Peter van Inwagen, 277–313. Grand Rapids: Eerdmans, 2004.

Oord, Thomas Jay. "Essay in Pluriform Love." *Process Perspectives* 43 (2022) 4–8.

———. *God Can't: How to Believe in God and Love after Tragedy, Abuse, and Other Evils*. Grasmere, ID: SacraSage, 2019.

Orlinsky, H. "Nationalism-Universalism and Internationalism in Ancient Israel." In *Translating and Understanding the Old Testament: Essays in Honor of Herbert Gordon May*, edited by Harry Thomas Frank and William L. Reed, 206–36. Nashville: Abingdon, 1970.

Otto, Rudolf. *The Idea of the Holy: An Inquiry into the non-rational factor in the idea of the divine and its relation to the rational*. New York: Oxford University Press, 1958. First published in 1923.

Owens, John Joseph. *Analytical Key to the Old Testament; volume 3: Ezra–Song of Solomon*. Grand Rapids: Baker, 1991.

Painter, Nell Irvin. *Sojourner Truth: A Life, a Symbol*. New York: Norton, 1996.

Plantinga, Alvin. "The Free Will Defense." In *The Problem of Evil: Selected Readings*, edited by Michael L. Peterson, 103–33. Library of Religious Philosophy 8. Notre Dame: University of Notre Dame Press, 1992.

Pope, Marvin H. *Job Introduction, Translation, and Notes*. Anchor Bible 15. Garden City, NY: Doubleday, 1973.

Rad, Gerhard von. *Old Testament Theology, Volume I: The Theology of Israel's Historical Traditions*. Translated by D. M. G. Stalker. Old Testament Library. Louisville: Westminster John Knox, 2001. Originally, Munich: Christian Kaiser Verlag, 1957.

Ragaz, Leonhard. "God Himself Is the Answer." In *The Dimensions of Job: A Study and Selected Readings*, edited by Nahum N. Glatzer, 128–31. Eugene, OR: Wipf and Stock, 2002. Original source: Ragaz, *Die Bibel: Eine Deutung* (Zurich: Diana Verlag, 1947–50).

Renan, Ernest. "The Cry of the Soul." In *The Dimensions of Job: A Study and Selected Readings*, edited by Nahum N. Glatzer, 111–23. Eugene, OR: Wipf and Stock, 2002. Original source: Renan, *Le Livre de Job* (Paris: Calmann Lévy, 1859).

Rowley, H. H. "The Intellectual Versus the Spiritual Solution." In *The Dimensions of Job: A Study and Selected Readings*, edited by Nahum N. Glatzer, 123–28. Eugene, OR: Wipf and Stock, 2002. Original source: Rowley, *From Moses to Qumran: Studies in the Old Testament* (New York: Association Press, 1963).

Saadiah. *The Book of Theodicy: Translation and Commentary on the Book of Job by Saadiah ben Joseph al-Fayyumi*. Translated by L. E. Goodman. Yale Judaica Series XXV. New Haven: Yale University Press, 1988.

Schneider, John R. "Seeing God Where the Wild Things Are: An Essay on the Defeat of Horrendous Evil." In *Christian Faith and the Problem of Evil*, edited by Peter van Inwagen, 226–62. Grand Rapids: Eerdmans, 2004.

Seow, C. L. *Job 1–21: Interpretation and Commentary*. Grand Rapids: Eerdmans, 2013.

Suriano, Matthew J. "Death, Disinheritance, and Job's Kinsman-Redeemer." *JBL* 129 (2010) 49–66.

Sutherland, Robert. *Putting God on Trial: The Biblical Book of Job*. Kindle ed. Victoria, British Columbia: Trafford, 2004.

Teilhard de Chardin, Pierre. *The Future of Man*. Translated by Norman Denny. New York: Harper & Row: 1964. Original: Paris: Editions du Seuil, 1959.

———. *Human Energy*. Translated by J. M. Cohen. London: Collins, 1969. Original:, Paris: Editions du Seuil, 1962.

———. *Let Me Explain*. Texts selected and arranged by Jean-Pierre Demoulin. Translated by René Hague and others. New York: Harper & Row, 1966.

———. *Toward the Future*. Translated by René Hague. New York: Harcourt Brace Jovanovich, 1975. Originally, Paris: Editions du Seuil, 1973.

Terrien, Samuel L. "Job as a Sage." In *The Sage in Israel and the Ancient Near East*, edited by John G. Gammie and Leo G. Perdue, 231–42. Winona Lake, IN: Eisenbrauns, 1990.

———. *Job*. NCBC. Nashville: Nelson, 1970.

Tilley, Terence W. *The Evils of Theodicy*. Eugene, OR: Wipf and Stock, 2000. Original: Washington, DC: Georgetown University Press, 1991.

———. "Reply to Nagasawa." In *The Problem of Evil: Eight Views in Dialogue*, edited by N. N. Trakakis, 197–99. Oxford: Oxford University Press, 2018.

———. "A Trajectory of Positions." In *The Problem of Evil: Eight Views in Dialogue*, edited by N. N. Trakakis, 176–90. Oxford: Oxford University Press, 2018.

Timmer, Daniel. "God's Speeches, Job's Responses, and the Problem of Coherence in the Book of Job: Sapiential Pedagogy Revisited." *CBQ* 71 (2009) 286–305.

Vanhoozer, Kevin J. *First Theology: God, Scripture, and Hermeneutics*. Downers Grove, IL: InterVarsity, 2002.

Vicchio, Stephen J. *The Book of Job: A History of Interpretation and a Commentary*. Eugene, OR: Wipf and Stock, 2020.

West, Mona. "Irony in the Book of Jonah: Audience Identification with the Hero." *Perspectives in Religious Studies* 11 (1984) 233–42.

Whedbee, William. "The Comedy of Job." *Semeia* 7 (1977) 1–39.

Whybray, Roger Norman. *Job*. Readings: A New Bible Commentary. Sheffield, UK: Sheffield Academic, 1998.

Winkelmann, Carol. "'In the Bible, It Can Be So Harsh!' Battered Women, Suffering, and the Problem of Evil." In *Christian Faith and the Problem of Evil*, edited by Peter van Inwagen, 148–84. Grand Rapids: Eerdmans, 2004.

Wolterstorff, Nicholas. *Lament for a Son*. Grand Rapids: Eerdmans, 1987.

Subject Index

Subject Index

Name Index

Including deities

Abraham, 20, 31, 70, 74

Adam, 73

Adams, Marilyn McCord, 12, 81

Adams, Victoria, 4, 58–59, 73, 86

Andersen, Francis I., 4, 6, 8, 10, 15,
18–21, 24, 30, 32, 35–36,
49–50, 52, 63, 66–67

Anderson, Bradford A., 8–9

Anselm of Canterbury, 82

Aquinas. *See* Thomas Aquinas

Arundi, Isaac, 59

Ashurbanipal, 3

Augustine, 82

Baillie, John, 82–83

Baker, Sharon L., 92–93

Barr, Stephen M., 82

Belitsos, Byron, 67, 86, 90

Berdyaev, Nicolas, 81

Bernard of Clairvaux, 16

Bildad, 20–21, 26–27, 34–35, 99–
101, 103, 106, 110

Boss, Jeffrey, 8, 14, 19–20, 23, 26, 28,
34, 38, 51, 62, 68–69, 73, 76

Brown, Francis; Driver, and Briggs,
54, 62

Browning, Robert, 24, 83–84

Brueggemann, Walter, 40

Buber, Martin, 16

Cannon, Dale, 82

Castelo, Daniel, 92, 95

Clines, David J. A., 2, 29, 40, 52

Crenshaw, James L., 9

Curtis, J. B., 40

Dahood, Mitchell, 30

Dhorme, E., 30, 49, 62

Driver, S. R., 31

Echeverria, Eduardo J., 93–94

Eisen, Robert, 58–60, 69

Ekstrom, Laura Waddell, 89–90

El, 6, 51, 55, 61

El Shaddai or Shaddai, 6, 51, 55, 61

Elihu, 1–3, 67, 29, 35, 39–58,
60–62, 69, 78–82, 95–97, 99,
103–11

Elijah, 40, 106

Eliphaz, 8, 17, 21, 26, 32–33, 41, 45,
4749, 68, 79, 99–100, 103,
106, 109–10

Elohim, 6, 15, 51, 55, 70

Ephrem the Syrian, 30

Erickson, Amy, 27–29, 30

Fishbane, Michael, 46

Girard, René, 71

Good, Edwin M., 2, 19, 35, 37, 40,
53, 64

Goodheart, Eugene, 89

Name Index

Gordis, Robert, 8, 40, 63
Gregory the Great, 2
Guillaume, Philippe, 25, 69, 71

Hartley, John E., 2, 44, 46–49, 51, 54, 63
Haught, John F., 90
Hays, Christopher, 4–5, 12–24, 37
Hick, John, 91
Hitler, Adolf, 88
Höffding, Harald, 24
Holladay, William L., 54, 68

Ibn Tibbon, 59
Inwagen, Peter van, 86–87

Janzen, J. Gerald, 24, 30–31, 40, 63
Jerome, 30
Jesus, 28, 30, 91–96
Job's wife, 11, 16, 38, 99–100, 103
John Chrysostom, 30
John Paul II, Pope, 93
Joo, Samantha, 68
Jung, Carl Gustav, 75–77

Kaufmann, U. Milo, 10
Kaufmann, Yehezkel, 6, 35, 53, 79
Keats, John 90
Kynes, Bill, 16–20, 31, 39, 44, 67, 78
Kynes, Will, 16–20, 31, 39, 44, 67, 78

LaCocque, André, 65, 70–71
Leibniz, Gottfried Wilhelm, 12
Linafelt, Tod, 40

Maimonides, 58–59
Marduk, 3
Margulies, Zachary, 3–5, 38–39
McClelland, Richard T., 88–89
McGrew, Israel, 7
Moberly, R. Walter L., 13
Moltmann, Jürgen, 91, 94–95
Moore, Michael S., 4–5, 9, 13, 15, 17
Moses, 30

Newsom, Carol A., 2, 13, 24, 26–27, 40–41, 57, 62, 66

Oesterley, W. O. E., 67
Omolade, Barbara, 81
Oord, Thomas Jay, 87–88
Orlinsky, H., 84
Otto, Rudolf, 72
Owens, John Joseph, 49

Painter, Nell Irvin, 81
Pascal, Blaise, 82
Plantinga, Alvin, 12, 86
Plato, 10
Pope, Marvin H., 3–4, 6, 14, 21, 23, 25–27, 29–30, 34, 36, 38, 54, 61–62, 66–68, 73
Purrington, Mr., 76

Ra, 5
Rad, Gerhard von, 5
Ragaz, Leonhard, 80
Rashi, 15, 22, 73
Renan, Ernest, 30
Robinson, T. H., 67
Rowley, H. H., 22, 26, 33, 67, 72, 80

Saadiah, 33, 52, 57–58
Satan, the satan, 1–2, 11, 13, 15–16, 69, 71, 75–76, 100, 107
Schneider, John R., 66
Seow, C. L., 13
Simon ben Ẓemaḥ Duran, 69
Sojourner Truth, 81
Solomon, 6
Stevenson, W. B., 34
Suriano, Matthew J., 27–29
Sutherland, Robert, 40, 72–75

Teilhard de Chardin, Pierre, 96
Terrien, Samuel L., 8
Thomas Aquinas, 30
Tilley, Terence W., 11–12
Timmer, Daniel, 64, 68–69, 75

Ancient Documents Index